GOLDEN THREADS.

GOLDEN THREADS

SELECTED STORIES.

BY
MRS. HELEN C. KNIGHT
AND OTHERS.

How fast the shuttle flies,
Weaving the web of life!
The Golden Threads of love and duty
Endue it with immortal beauty.

EDITED BY
CHARLES J. DOE.

A PUBLICATION OF

CURIOSMITH

MINNEAPOLIS,
2009.

Published by Curiosmith.
P. O. Box 390293, Minneapolis, Minnesota, 55439.
Internet: curiosmith.com.
E-mail: shopkeeper@curiosmith.com.

Printed and bound in the United States of America.

Golden Threads is a book of moral stories, narratives, and poems first published in the middle of the nineteenth century. The cover art and illustrations are renditions of that edition.

Library of Congress Control Number: 2008942164

ISBN 978-0-9817505-3-8

CONTENTS.

CONTENTS. (CONTINUED)

CONTENTS. (CONTINUED)

IS IT FATHER'S LETTER?

GEORGE was at home from college, and much did he have to tell about college life, the professors, the boys' pranks, boarding in commons, studies, exercises: "And, mother," he said one evening, "there's a club of fellows in college that don't believe the Bible as *you* do. They say it is absurd to call it the word of God. They say it isn't any more divine than Herodotus, or Pliny, or any of those old authors. It's only history, like any history, but not inspired by God." George enlarged freely upon this new set of opinions, new at least to him, but old as the world is, for Satan's great aim in Paradise was to destroy Eve's faith in the word of God; and he has never slackened his efforts to do so with men ever since. His mother saw that her son's faith was shocked, if not shaken; at any rate, that worst of all evils, doubts, like a flock of carrion crows, had been lodged in his mind.

While they were talking, one of the bank clerks handed in a letter. "From father!" cried George, holding it up, "and postmarked Chicago." "From father, from father!" shouted the younger children, clapping their hands. It was for mother, but she bade George open and read it aloud. A long and interesting letter it was to this little family group, and they all began to talk at once about its contents as soon as George had finished, all but mother, who amid this hubbub of cheery voices said nothing; she sat gravely looking into the fire. At last, when they began to wonder at her silence, she said, "I doubt if that letter *is* from your father." The children looked at each other and at their mother in surprise. For a moment no one spoke; the glad flow of their spirits seemed suddenly checked and chilled.

"Why, mother, it has certainly got father's signature," said James, taking up the letter and looking it over. "Anybody might know his signature; it's exactly the same he writes on his bank-bills—just such a quirl of the G, just such square Ws; that says it's father's as clear as daylight." "In other words, proves it authentic," said the young collegian George.

"And certainly there's no denying father's seal on the out-side," said Jessie, taking her turn at the letter, "the eagle with a scroll in his mouth, the very one Judge Halmer gave him so long ago."

"Why, mother," cried a third, "it *suits* us so. Who but father, away off in Chicago, knows you have a son George in college? Who but father knew Sarah wanted a writing-desk? Who but father knew all about poor Jessie's lame leg? Who in all that big Chicago knows all our different wants, and could say just the things *to* us and *about* us all, but *father,* our own father dear?"

"Well, mother, I reckon you won't doubt when the desk and your shawl and all the little knickknacks father mentions having sent, *come.* That will be convincing enough, I guess," said George pretty positively.

The conversation passed off, but not the impression it left on George's mind, which was an uneasy one. How strange, he thought, for his mother to doubt, and so seriously doubt, whether that letter was from his father. Was his mother going crazy? Could this be a symptom of insanity? He knew she had not been well, and two or three people were in the Insane hospital that once were just as unlikely to be there as his mother. He pondered the matter long after he went to bed, and fell asleep painfully puzzled.

The next night the thundering knock of the express-man

announced the arrival of father's promised package. "There, mother," said George, as he received and opened it, taking out one after the other the articles specified in the letter, "does not *this* confirm father's letter?" After they had been sufficiently admired and talked over, George sat down by his mother, and affectionately taking her hand, "Now, dear mother," he asked, "what did make you doubt it was father's letter? It seemed to me so extraordinary."

"Not more extraordinary, my son, than for one to doubt the genuineness of the word of God, the Bible, the heavenly Father's letter to us." Then George instantly saw it was to teach him an important lesson. "How did you all try to prove your father's letter genuine, that he was indeed the author of it; what was the proof?" she asked.

He thought a moment, and then answered, "First by his signature; then by his seal; then because it suited our case; and tonight, by the arrival of the package, which it *said* he sent; that is, by the fulfillment of its promises—four substantial proofs, mother."

"And these are precisely some of the proofs which satisfy us that the Bible is from God," said his mother. "First, it *professes* to be; its writers declare it is so. God said to Moses when he sent him with his messages, 'I will be thy mouth.' David says, 'The Spirit of the Lord spake by me, and his word was in my tongue.' When Christ sent his disciples to preach the gospel, he told them, 'It is not ye that speak, but the Spirit of your Father which speaketh in you.' You see it professes to be from God; his *signature* is put to it.

"That alone is not enough, however. Let us look further, and we shall find God's *seal* upon it. Moses went to Egypt with a message from God. 'Prove that it is from God,' they said. And what did he do? He wrought miracles before them. '*There* are my credentials,' he said." "What are credentials?" asked James. "That which gives us a *title* to people's confidence," answered his mother. "When a man is sent to this country from England on the Queen's business, he brings his credentials with him—a letter with the English seal upon it. The apostles in the same way wrought miracles in proof that they brought the gospel from God. Miracles are God's *seal* upon his messages to man.

"Then you said your father's letter *suited our case*," continued she; "it knew all about us. And this is a great proof that the Bible is from God; it is so suited to our wants. We are guilty, it offers pardon. We are rebels against God's law, it brings a message of peace. We are lost, it tells us of a Savior. We are dead, its truths bring life and immortality to light. We are sorrowful and wretched, it promises joy and hope and heaven. The Bible is wonderfully adapted to all our wants, you see. It knows our case.

"And the further proof is, *what it says comes to pass* in the fulfillment of its promises and prophecies. The arrival of the package you considered the crowning proof of the genuineness of your father's letter. In a like manner the Bible promises, and no one yet ever found it to fail. It foretells future events, not for one year only, but years and centuries beforehand—events which none but God's all-seeing eye could foresee and foreknow. In the march of time they all come to pass, and are constantly fulfilling before our eyes.

"Therefore you see, my son, that the same kind of evidence which established the genuineness of your father's letter, and which you thought it so extraordinary that I could doubt, establishes the genuineness of God's message to man; and none but unfair or frivolous minds, incapable of appreciating evidence, will ever doubt or reject the truth that *the Scriptures are the word of God*, written, as they declare, that we might believe that Jesus is the Christ, the Son of God, and that believing we might have life through his name. To find this life, the *one great* object and end of all our endeavors, George, 'Search the Scriptures,' says the Son of God; and it is a search we cannot too earnestly make."

"Oh, mother," said the young collegian the next day, kissing her pale cheek, "your words are like apples of gold in pictures of silver."

NUMBER ONE.

"I ALWAYS take care of number one," said one of a troop of boys, at the end of a bridge, some wanting to go one way and some another.

"That's *you*, out and out," cried one of his companions. "You don't think or care about anyone but yourself; you ought to be called Number One." "If I did not take care of Number One, who *would*, I should like to know?" cried he.

True, Number One was right. He ought to take care of himself—*good care*. "But does not that smack a little of selfishness?" the boys ask. "Number One thinks of nobody but himself." Nobody *but* himself! That certainly is selfish, and therefore wrong. Yet Number One is committed to our own care. What sort of care? is the all-important question.

The care of his soul. Number One has a soul to save from sin and from hell. Number One has a soul to win to Christ, to holiness, and to heaven. Here is a great work to do.

Take care of his habits. Make Number One industrious, persevering, self-denying, and frugal. Give him a plenty of good healthy work to do, and teach him how best to do it. Keep Number One from the beer-bottle, the whiskey-jug, the wine-cup. Keep him from gambling, betting, dice, and cards. Keep him from loafing, and all idle company.

Take care of the lips of Number One. Let truth dwell on them. Put a bridle in his mouth, that no angry, backbiting tale shall come from it. Let no profane word escape. Let the law of kindness rule his tongue, and all his conversation be such as becomes a child of God.

Take care of the affections and feelings of Number One. Teach him to love God with all his heart, and his neighbor as himself. To care for others, and share with others. To be lowly in mind, forgiving, gentle, sympathizing, willing to bear and forbear, easily entreated, doing good as he has opportunity, and full of good works.

This is the care to take of Number One, and a rich blessing will he prove to his home and neighborhood and himself. Boys, you all have Number One to take care of; and a responsible charge it is. Remember, also, there is a day of reckoning, when you will be called to render an account of your charge of him at the bar of God.

IN THE WOODS.

~~

"TOM JONES is serious," said one boy to another. "Serious! Is his mother going to frighten him into religion? He needn't be scared; he won't die yet."

"I suppose religion is as good to live by as to die by."

"If we are happy enough now, what's the use of being long-faced, and troubling ourselves about religion till we get older."

"*Are* we happy enough, Bill? I a'n't. I could be a great deal happier. I have a great deal of 'not satisfied' feeling *here,*" said the boy, pressing his hand on his bosom, "which I expect religion could fill up, only I don't know how to get it."

"I am sure *I* can't tell you how," said his companion. They stopped, jumped over a stone wall, and the talk died away in the field on the other side.

Thomas Jones *was* serious. The Holy Spirit had visited this boy and showed him his secret faults, and he saw them clearer than he ever saw them before. He felt that he was very far from God. He was afraid of God. It seemed to him as if he had lost his way in the woods on a dark day. He was troubled; he could not find the way out. He certainly felt very heavy-hearted. His minister told him about repenting, and his mother told him about praying to Jesus, and he tried to follow their directions. But he got neither light nor comfort. Often he went out and sat down at the foot of an old oak-tree behind the barn, and thought.

"Mother," said he one day, "doesn't the Bible talk about 'striving' and 'seeking?' It seems to me as if I am 'seeking' and 'striving' to find forgiveness and comfort, but I can't."

"The Bible never speaks of heartfelt and earnest 'seeking' without 'finding,' or 'striving' without 'entering in,'" answered his mother; "and we have no Bible reason for supposing that the one does not in all cases, sooner or later, follow the other.

To think otherwise, would be to suppose God less willing to receive us and make us happy than we are to go to him."

"Well, mother—" Thomas stopped; he did not exactly know how to state his case.

"'Come unto me, all ye that labor and are heavy-laden, and I will give you rest.' The Lord gives that invitation," said his mother.

"But maybe he don't mean *me*," answered the boy.

"The Lord says again, '*Him* that cometh to me I will in no wise cast out.' That is to you, my child. Can't you take the Lord at his word? Prove him now, and see if he fails to keep his word."

Taking the Lord at his word—that struck Thomas' mind. Could he not take Him at his word? He could trust his father's word, and his mother's word; should he not trust God's word as well? Thomas went down into the barn, and he fell on his knees and made a short prayer, something like this: "O Lord, I am in the dark; I want light; I want comfort; I want to love thee; I want to be good." This was his prayer in the morning. At noon, after he came from school, he went again and offered the same prayer. He ate his dinner, and went to school again. He did not feel that his prayer was answered. After school, he was down at the foot of the old oak-tree, offering the same prayer still. The next day it was pretty much the same, except that Thomas, instead of getting discouraged, prayed more in earnest than ever. It seemed as if he was really taking God at his word. He did not feel like going back, but forward.

But *did* God answer him? If you had asked him that question at the end of the second day after he began to pray so, he would have shaken his head. He still felt himself in the dark woods of his sins.

The next morning, when he waked, a little sunbeam shined into the top of his window on the opposite wall. "What a beautiful sunbeam!" thought Thomas. "It comes from the good sun, shining to make day for us. It is *God's* sun. I love the sunbeam." Then he heard a little robin sing on the tree. "Dear robin," thought Thomas. "God made the robin. How sweetly it sings. It is singing to God's ear." And Thomas loved robins, he was sure he did. Then he turned his eye, and caught a glimpse of the blue sky through the trees. "There's heaven," thought Thomas. "How beautiful heaven must be, where Christ and the angels are." And Thomas was so glad, looking up to the sky and thinking of his Savior and heaven. Thomas was as happy as could be; he loved everything he saw. He arose, and falling down on his knees he praised God. God was no longer far off; he was very near. He was no longer afraid. His heart was full of love. He felt as if the Son of God had him by the hand, and was leading him to his Father in heaven.

Then Thomas felt that his prayer was answered. He was out of the woods. He felt it was so sweet to be forgiven, and have God's peace in his bosom.

This was the beginning of a boy's Christian life. The Bible calls it being "born again." "The wind bloweth where it listest, and thou hearest the sound thereof, but canst not tell whence it cometh, or whither it goeth; so is every one that is born of the Spirit;" that is, one cannot explain it; he only knows it *is so,* from a happy experience in his own bosom.

This is a specimen of that religion which makes people happy, because it brings forgiveness of sin, and peace and love to the soul. These things *satisfy* the soul, and nothing else will.

AMOS AND HIS BOSSY.

NEVER did I feel prouder or richer than when father said, "Amos, I guess I shall give you Bossy; that calf shall be called yours." He was mending a yoke in old barn door, while I his eldest boy was watching Bossy's frisky movements in the yard. Bossy behaved as if it was a very pleasant thing to have four nimble legs to caper round with. And so it is. Much as I loved her before, after father said this I loved her a great deal better. "Nep," I said, "Nep, that's *my* calf; see that you don't dog her." Nep wagged his tail as much as to say, "I understand." To my five younger brothers and sisters I was not slow in telling the news that "Bossy was *my* calf; father said so."

"Mother," I cried, "please look out the window and see this calf. Well, she's *mine*. Bossy is mine." "Nice calf," answered mother, peeping pleasantly out of the dairy window; "I suppose you will let me churn your butter for you." "Hurrah! Yes, mother," I shouted at the funny thought. We had the "old cow," Bossy's mother, "Star," a two years' old heifer, and Bossy; besides these, our barn-yard contained a yoke of oxen, a horse, a few sheep, and plenty of fowls. These, with six children, make quite a family to be stabled and fed at our small hill-side farm.

The next person to be informed of my good news was Joshua Pepper. Joshua and I were schoolmates, always on the best of terms. School did not keep then, and his farm was three miles off. However, I made out to see him, and squatting down under the old ash in his pasture, I set him guessing out my good fortune. "Well," he said, after many unsuccessful attempts, "if 'tisn't a new knife, I'll give up. Tell me." "No, no," I cried, rois-teringly, "no. It is a *calf*, our Boss. Father gave it to me. It's *mine*, old fellow." "*Yours*, Amos!" he looked delightfully incredu-lous. "Why, it's real good in your father. I suppose you know I

got a lamb. And now, Amos"—he stopped, and twitched me by the sleeve, as if a great thought was striking him—"will the calf's calves be yours? That's it. Will Bossy's Bossies be yours too? You'll have a drove soon, Amos." Respect and admiration twinkled in his little grey eyes as he glanced at me: "Yes, a *drove* soon." "I shall; sha'n't I? A drove!" I cried, starting on my feet. "Now have it understood," said Joshua with a knowing and confidential look. "Tell him, as Boss is yours, her calves will be yours too, no mistake." "I will, that's a fact," feeling in full force that two heads are better than one.

No time offered to settle this important item until the next morning, when I tumbled out of bed by daylight, and bounded into the kitchen, where the fire was already snapping on the hearth. "Father," I shouted lustily. He had gone to the barn.

"Father," I cried, scampering after him with my trousers half on, "father, will Bossy's children be mine or yours? Can't my calf's calves be *mine,* father?" "We'll see about that when the time comes," he answered quietly, and as quietly milking on. "Well, father, but if Bossy is mine, I don't see why her calves ar'n't mine, all Bossy's cows. They are mine; are they not, father?" "Perhaps so; but better wait till they come, Amos." Father's "perhaps so" was about equivalent to "yes;" therefore I immediately felt myself the master of a drove, a fine drove of fat cattle, for my boyish fancies were as vivid as my eyes were large. I longed to race over the hills and tell Joshua. As that could not be, I contented myself with strutting round Boss, patting her sides, examining her flanks, until altogether forget-ting the dignity fit to the master of a drove, I suddenly threw my arms round her neck and kissed her. In coquettish surprise, Bossy kicked up her heels, and switching her tail, I was quite willing to let go of her. The rest of the day was spent in gener-ous appropriations of my prospective stock. Every brother and sister should have a pick—a calf to one, and a calf to another, theirs to *keep,* as mine was. And in these affluent circumstances I continued for several days, as rich, generous, and happy as one need be.

One day, not many weeks after, father sent me into the field with a basket of potatoes to plant, himself soon to follow. I was to drop, and he to cover them. Away I went, and to work I went, dropping, dropping, dropping, until the basket was empty. No father. Where was he? I cut across the potato-patch, and ran home for the hoe in order to finish the work myself. In the yard I found a man, the very man father always tried to dodge so, and Bossy with a halter round her neck, on the point of being led off. When father saw me, he turned and went into the barn. "What you going to do with her?" I asked, as the man jerked Bossy along. He looked back, but made no answer. "What you carrying my calf off for?" I angrily demanded, marching after him. "Your calf!" he said, sneeringly. "Yes, it is *my* calf; father said so." "Your calf!" he repeated, and I shall never forget his tones. "What you leading her off for?" I cried, as he drew her further and further down the hill; "she don't want to go." "'Tisn't as *she* says, I reckon," said the man in a surly tone. To rush back and ask father what this all meant, was to lose sight of Bossy, and to lose sight of Bossy could not be thought of. "Where you going to take Bossy?" I savagely demanded, my courage rising with the emergency. *"She's mine!"* "She's not yours, youngster," said the man; "she's Mr. Gibbs'. I've just taken her for a debt. I'm the sheriff, and I shall seize you soon if you don't behave;" and quickening his pace, he tugged Bossy after him.

The sheriff, that unaccountable man, so mysteriously con- nected with the disappearance from time to time of pigs from the pen, lambs from the fold, and fowls from their roost. The sheriff! I stood still, afraid to go on, yet straining my eyes after Bossy. As she was about to make a turn in the road, I cried excitedly, "Bossy, Bossy!" Bossy pricked up her ears and turned round her head. The man gave the halter a jerk, and both disappeared behind the trees, leaving poor me in a burst of passionate sorrow and bitter disappointment.

A little over it, I went in quest of mother. She was in the bed- room. "My dear boy," she said piteously, well divining my feelings. The children soon came running in, but she hushed them away, and we were alone. "Mother," I at length asked, breaking the sorrowful silence, "what business had that man with my Bossy?" "He took her for a debt which your poor father could not pay," she answered sadly. "And can they take any thing for a debt?" I asked anxiously. "Even the house over our heads," she said. "And turn us all out of doors?" "Yes, Amos, though I pray God it may never come to that," said she. "Then I will *never, never, never get into debt,"* I cried, "if they can take all you like best to pay for it;" and Bossy's dear image again brought tears to my eyes. It was some time before I could join father in the potato-field, and when I did, neither of us spoke. Father looked unhappy, and I minded he did not always seem to know what he was doing.

I could not go to pasture that night. Ben and Neptune

fetched home the cows. Neither could I trust myself in the barnyard, nor could I relish my bread and milk, for it was Bossy's mother's milk. Just before going to bed, I crept round the barn and peeped through the fence. There was the old cow, and there "Star," chewing their evening cud in sorrowful loneliness. Poor Bossy, the thought of *her* whereabouts was too much for me, and I made good an escape to my humble quarters in the garret.

This was my first experience of a debt, and it made its mark on me. I resolved never to get into the hands of a sheriff. If my earnings are not always equal to my wants—and a great many of our wants are fancied wants—*"do without"* is my motto. *"Deny thyself"* is the true principle. When I see young men, and even boys, running up cigar bills, oyster bills, stable bills, bills for dress, I say, Young man, you are on the road to ruin. Begin the habit of running in debt, and it is hard to break it. It will be worse than a chain-cable dragging you down. It will damage your integrity, and make you a mean, dishonest, and lying fellow.

True, I kept clear from money debts; but by and by I found out there were debts of another kind to pay—debts of obedience and gratitude to God, of love and good-will to my neighbor. Had I paid *these?* Alas, no. My conscience enlightened, said *no,* and condemned me. I felt bad indeed, very bad, for I saw it was a long account, and I had nothing to pay it with in the great day of reckoning. There I saw who Jesus Christ was, and what he had done.

> "The ever blessed Son of God
>   Went up to Calvary for me;
> There paid my debt, there bore my load,
>   In his own body on the tree."

He could blot out may sad score of sins with his own blood. I fell at his feet, and prayed for his help. I found him good security. His word is sure.

STRIKE WHEN THE IRON'S HOT.

❧

THE old smith always said to us, as we used to gather round his anvil in the old shop, on our way to and from school—"Strike when the iron's hot, boys," as, suiting his action to his words, he raised his brawny arm and dealt the swift and heavy blows upon the glowing iron. "Mind ye, boys, there are always redhot minutes in life, when you must ply the strokes; if you let them cool, you may hammer for ever, and never do anything. Strike when the iron's hot, boys. Remember that."

It is a small piece, but it carries a tremendous charge; and on me it made a strong impression. I was anxious to get an education, but my father was poor, and neither he nor my mother favored the idea; indeed they were against it. Years of study, and no means to carry me through looked dismal enough to them. But I was determined to compass it, if possible, and therefore studied and worked with all my might.

One day, as I was building the fire in Col. Jones' office, "Well, Dick," said he, "I hear you mean to go to college." "Yes, sir," said I. "Tough struggle for a poor boy," said he. "Yes, sir," I answered; "but boys have gone through it." "Are you ready to enter college?" he asked. "No, sir; there's no good chance here; I want to go a year to —— academy." "Can you manage to get on the charity list there, Dick? If you can, why, maybe we can give you a lift," said the colonel. "Thank you, sir," said I.

"Strike when the iron's hot," said I to myself; and as soon as I had finished my work in the colonel's office, I went to my minister, got a recommendation wrote to the principal of the —— academy, and asked if my name could be put on the charity foundation—a fund which this school had to pay the board of a certain number of poor scholars of good character and respect- able talents. As a good Providence would have it, in two days I received an answer from the principal, telling me to be on hand the next week. I took the letter to the colonel. "Whew, Dick," said he, on reading it, "I didn't expect such dispatch as this." "It's best to strike when the iron's hot, sir," said I. "Go ahead, Dick," cried the colonel; "you *will* go ahead. Come in tonight, and I'll look up my offer."

The way clear, I told my parents; for if the way were clear, they had no objections; and so I started on my course of education, and the motto which started me pretty well helped me through. I studied law. Where to settle, was the question—go west, go south, stay at home, or *where?* There was no lack of lawyers in any direction, it seemed to me; and as for openings, I pretty nearly concluded that an opening was just where one was ready to work. "Why not try it in N——?" said a friend one day; "I hear Thompson is about leaving." Thompson was a rising lawyer in N——, a neighboring town. That night I took a chaise,* and started for the place. The next morning I saw Thompson, en- gaged his office, and before night I was as good as settled. The week following five other lawyers came to inquire about Mr. Thompson's leaving and to take his stand, provided the report was true. "Striking when the iron's hot" put me into it; and fidelity to the principle has carried me much further on the road to success, since my settlement in business, than my most san- guine hopes ever looked for.

That's it, boys; don't let slip *present opportunity* for doing or getting all the good you can. As Shakespeare expresses it,

> "There is a tide in the affairs of men,
> Which, taken at the flood, leads on to fortune;
> Omitted, all the voyage of their life
> Is bound in shallows and in miseries;
> And we must take the current when it serves,
>   Or lose our ventures."

---

*Chaise—a two wheel carriage.

And, boys, if this is true in the common business of life, it is no less true in the business which the soul transacts with its Maker. There are seasons in our religious history big with the most solemn consequences—awfully critical moments, when our condition for eternity seems to vibrate on the decision and the action of a moment. Your conscience is tender; the Spirit of God is striving with you; the voice of duty is clearly heard, and the path of duty is clearly seen; Christ is near you: these are golden moments—turning-points in our religious history, when to seize them brings us out of the darkness of sin and temptation, into the clear shining of God's providence and grace; while neglect of them may hush the voice of conscience, blind the eye to eternity, and turn the soul from its Savior into all the helplessness of sin and unbelief, from which we may never extricate ourselves. Above all things boys, "strike for the *right,* when the iron's hot."

THE JAIL-CHAMBER.

"SHALL we take that poor child?" asked Mr. Stone, as the family sat at breakfast. "He is a bad boy, I suspect."

"My greatest fear is his influence over our children," said Mrs. Stone. "On *their* account we may well hesitate."

"Might not our children help to improve him?" asked the father, looking round on his five little ones in their blue aprons, eating their bread and milk.

"I'll be his brother," said Willie, "and let him fly my kite."

"He is a little heathen, from all I can hear," said Mr. Stone. "I don't know as we can make much of him."

"But, father, we send missionaries to the heathen; and if we expect one Christian can do a great many heathen good, can't a good many Christians do one heathen good, and he not a heathen either?" asked Susy.

"We'll *try*, Susy," said her father. "Jake shall come."

Who was Jake? He was the son of Mr. Stone's brother, a squatter out west, all whose family dying, this boy was left to be sent east to his father's relatives, and he was now on his way to Mr. Stone. Jake was about nine. In a few days he arrived. He was short, stubbed, and would have been handsome, only he seemed to think washing his face and combing his hair quite unnecessary. As for shoes, socks, or hat, he hated them. And he roved round the house and premises as lawless as a young buffalo on the prairies.

In these things he was gradually tamed; but more serious faults began to show themselves. He loved to torment his cousins. Dogged in his disposition, he sometimes broke into violent fits of temper, when he would destroy everything within his reach. Whipping had no effect; coaxing or reasoning had none. He did not care. That was the worst of it—*he didn't care.* Mr. and Mrs.

Stone did their best to improve him. They pitied the poor child with a real father's and mother's pity. They thought, *If our Willie was so;* and that made them bear and forbear with him.

He liked to tease his cousins, especially Susy. Susy was a gentle and delicate little girl, and she used to try in her small way to make poor Jake better, "because nobody *loves* him;" and nobody's loving him seemed to her the worst of his case. One day he got very angry with her, and in his rage threw her doll into the fire, tore her hair, and actually bit and scratched her arm until the blood came. What *was* to be done with Jake? What *could* be done with a boy who behaved more like a wild beast than a boy? His uncle said he must be locked up until he could promise better conduct.

There was a chamber in the house, once used as a nursery by some former family, which had iron slats across the two windows outside, and therefore was called the jail-chamber. It had little furniture in it, and was chiefly used as a sort of lumber-room. After setting his conduct faithfully before him, here they con-cluded to put Jake. He *"didn't care,"* he said. Jake was locked up the rest of the day, and all night; and perhaps nobody felt more sorry for him than Susy did.

"Mother," she said, "I can't go to sleep; I keep thinking of poor Jake, alone, and no light and nothing," and her little lip quivered.

It was the third day, and Jake showed no signs of sorrow for his fault. "Don't care," was all he condescended to say. "Mother," said Susy, "mayn't I go and be shut up, while Jake just comes out to see how pleasant 'tis? there is no sun there, nor anything."

The mother looked into the dear child's face, and said, "Go, Susy." Susy went to Jake's door, and unlocking it, said, "I asked mother if I might not come and take your place, Jake, for you to go out and see how pleasant 'tis; it is so, so very dismal here, and lonely." Jake looked up and stared at her. "You are a fool for 't," said he. He, however, walked slowly out, while Mrs. Stone came along and locked Susy in. "And let him eat dinner downstairs," whispered Susy, "and I'll eat *his* 'dinner'"

When Mr. Stone came home, his wife told him what had

happened. Jake took his seat at table opposite to Susy's vacant seat. "You can carry up Susy her bread and water," said Mrs. Stone, handing him the tray. He took it and walked away, looking very sober, if not softened. According to Susy's wish, he stayed downstairs all the afternoon and to supper.

"Must Susy stay there all night, if I don't?" he asked towards bedtime. "Yes," answered Mrs. Stone. Tears started in his eyes. He ran upstairs, and bolting into the jail-chamber, "Susy," he cried, "you are the best un I ever knowed. Susy, I'll never, never treat you so again. I'll never bite or scratch; no, never. I'm sorry, I am. I'll try to be a good boy, I will. Susy, what makes you so good to me?" and poor Jake cried as if his heart would break.

Jake was completely softened; and from that good hour he began in earnest to amend.

Children sometimes find it hard to understand what Jesus Christ has done for them. This little story illustrates it. We disobey God; we live unmindful of his laws and his kindness; we are hard-hearted, and our unlovely tempers and dispositions shut us out from God's dear family. The Son of God pities us; he loves us; he sees how unhappy sin has made us, and he came to set us free from its bondage, and to bring us back to the comforts, the joys, and the blessings of his Father's house; and he was willing to suffer for us—to suffer *in our stead,* in order to accomplish it. Read the gospel of St. John, and see there what he has done for you. What pity, what kindness, what love! Should it not melt our hearts, and make us truly desire, above all things else, to put away every sin, and to be meek and humble and good, like Jesus Christ himself?

THINKING OURSELVES OVER.

❧

"MOTHER, what is self-examination?" asked a child; "our superintendent said something about it, and he told us all to spend a little while every Sabbath practicing it—practicing *what*, mother?"

"Self-examination is *thinking ourselves over*," answered the mother. "You know how apt we are to forget ourselves, what we did and thought yesterday, and the day before, and the day before that. Now it is by calling to mind our past conduct that we can truly see it as it is, and improve upon it."

"*How* must I do, mother?" asked Mary; "tell me how to begin." Her mother said,

"You may first think over *your conduct towards your parents.* Have they had reason to find fault with you during the week; if so, what for? Have you disobeyed them or disputed with them, or been sullen or ill-humored towards them? And what good have you done them? Have you made them glad by your kindness, and your faithful and ready compliance with their wishes?

"Then think of *your duties to your brothers and sisters and little friends.* Ask yourself what has been your deportment towards them. How many have you made happier the last week? How many have you made unhappy? Have you spoken cross words to them? Have you been angry or ill-natured? Have you deceived them? What hard thoughts have you cherished in your heart towards them?"

"Oh, mother, it would take me a great while to think all that over, and I'm afraid," said the little girl, looking down—"I'm afraid it would not always please me. What next must I think of, mother?"

"*Faithfulness in your business.*" "Business!" said Mary, smiling; "papa has business; little girls hav'n't." "Oh, yes," said her mother, "any work which you have to do is your business—dusting the parlor, taking care of the baby, your studies at school; these are your employments, in which you ought to be diligent and faithful. Have you been? Do you never play in school? Do you thoroughly learn your lessons? Do you mind what the teacher says? Carefully think over whether your conduct is in all respects what a Christian child's should be." "I know a verse about business," said Mary; "the Bible tells us 'to be diligent in business, fervent in spirit, serving the Lord.' That means, we must mind God in it; doesn't it? What more is there to think over, mother?"

"*Secret faults*," answered she. "Have you cherished any wrong feelings in your heart? Have you had secret thoughts which you would be sorry to have exposed? Any envy of others—any pride? Have you harbored unkindness? Have you been selfish? Have you forgot God? Have you neglected to praise him, and to pray to him? Go over all this ground thoroughly, and confess your faults, and ask your Savior to make your heart clean, and help you to love only what is lovely."

"But Aunt Jane says there's no need of children's thinking," said Mary. "Without thinking," said Mary's mother, "there can be no improvement. Thoughtlessness is the besetting fault of youth. It is this which makes them giddy, foolish, and vain, and blinds them to their own defects."

Mary sat still for some time, looking out of the window. Then she came, and putting her arms around her mother's neck sweetly said, "Dear mother, I will try to be one of yours and God's good children."

To "think ourselves over" in this way is a very proper exercise for the Sabbath. Holy time is apt to seem long sometimes, because people do not know exactly how to spend it to the best account. Assign this duty a place somewhere; and if heartily and thoroughly taken up, it will be one of the greatest means of self-improvement. But while it is a *Sabbath* duty, is it not a week-day duty also? Every night, before you go to bed, and before you are too sleepy to remember, try and recall yourself for the day. Think what you have done right, and thank God for it. Think of the ways in which you have done wrong, and in which, if you are not careful, you will surely do wrong again. Name them in plain words in your prayers, and say, "Help me, O Lord," in such a thing, "that I may not again sin against thee."

THE ROYAL CHARTER.

GOING home! From the little boy, frightened to find himself out after dark, to the rough sailor on the sea, home is the bright spot ahead; and going home, the quickest way is best. A few months ago, a splendid steam-ship sailed from Australia bound home. England was home. She had a precious cargo, passengers and gold; three-hundred and eighty-six passengers, men, women, and little children. Husbands going home; fathers going home; young men going home; families going home; people who had been working hard in Australia to lay up money enough to *stay* at home. One gentleman had fifty thousand dollars in gold about him. And there was a crew of one hundred and twelve sailors, about as anxious to get home as the passengers were. The name of this ship was the Royal Charter, and her captain and officers were tried men.

From Australia to England, you know, is half round the world, but the Royal Charter made this voyage in a little less than two months. She was a brave ship. Oh, how glad they were to see the shores of old Ireland. She stopped in Cork harbor in the afternoon to land a few of her passengers, and here she telegraphed her safe arrival to her owners at London: for she thought herself as good as in; and the wires that evening told the good news to hundreds and hundreds of waiting and anxious hearts all over England.

What a quiet hubbub of delight was there on board. So near home. Nobody cares for any inconvenience now. Passengers long to pick out their luggage. Children are hushed with lullabys of "sweet home." Everybody is busy thinking, talking, planning what they shall do on landing. How rejoiced is everybody. The poor sea-sick ones almost smell the green earth again. And while the noble ship is steaming her way up the

Irish channel, her head towards Liverpool, the passengers meet in the cabin, after tea, to make congratulatory speeches, vote thanks to the captain and a beautiful silver service for his kindness and care through the voyage. The captain entered with hearty sympathy into the general joy, and gaily said that in less than twenty-four hours he expected to be sitting by his wife at home.

Bright and happy within, did they know the ship was already in the teeth of a terrible storm? The air was thick, the rain blinding, and the wind began to blow a hurricane. But the passengers; Oh they went to their berths as usual. There *was* a blow outside, but what mattered it? They were almost home. Meanwhile the ship, with bare poles, was put under full steam. She made Holyhead, within only three hours of Liverpool, when the storm began to master her. She no longer made head against the giant waves and angry winds, and began to drift, slowly drift towards the shore. It was pitch dark. Blue lights and rockets were sent up in hopes of attracting a pilot. Not a pilot-boat was out on that terrible sea. Minute guns of distress were fired. Nothing came to their help through the blinding storm. The night wore away and the gale increased. The cap- tain let go his anchors, but the cables that held them snapped asunder. He cut away his masts and rigging, but it gave the poor struggling ship no relief. At three o'clock in the morning she struck on the rocks, thumping, grinding, groaning. The affrighted passengers rushed to the cabin, with screams of terror and cries of mercy. Oh what a reunion!

What kind of shore they were on nobody knew. It was dark as midnight. No boat could live an instant on those angry billows. A tar-barrel was rigged to be set on fire in order to light up the coast, but every attempt to land was in vain. When day broke, the captain came below to calm the fright of his passen- gers and to assure them of safety. "We are on a sandy beach," he said cheerfully; "only a few yards from the shore; the tide will leave us dry: in ten minutes or more we shall be safe." *Could* he, in spite of the wild fury of the elements, make his promise good? Could he, in spite of the writhing, straining tim- bers, make his promise good? Could he? could he?

A sailor, with a rope tied round his waist, threw himself into the water and reached the land. Some fishermen, roused from their sleep, ran to the scene of disaster. A hawser was fastened to the rocks—a hawser, you know, is a large cable—a boat- swain's chair fastened to it, and in this way, by hauling it to and from the ship, several of the crew were safely landed; it was hoped all in the ship might be. The passengers were kept below, and kept quiet by constant promises of safety. *Could* they, *would* they be made good?

At seven the huge waves battered the poor groaning vessel with increasing fury, and she could hold out no longer. Sud- denly she snapped in two, and four hundred people, amid shrieks wilder than the shrieking storm, were crushed beneath her ruins. Never was destruction more complete. Her iron was torn to shreds and her wood ground to chips. In one hour not a vestige of the Royal Charter was to be seen. The captain went down with her. Perishing so near home! So near home!

Ah, there is One, and one only, who can make good his promises. There is One, and one only, who can save to the uttermost all who put their trust in him. This scene of peril brings to my mind perils no less terrible in their issue to crowds of the young around us, who are breasting wilder waves than the wild waves of the Irish channel—the waves of our ungodly life. People may cry, "Peace, peace," to you; but *sudden* destruction cometh upon you. They may again and again assure you of safety; but believe me, no one can promise you safety, and make his words *good*, but Christ the great Captain of our salvation. Cry to him, turn to him, cleave to him, and you will never perish *just outside* your heavenly home.

ALICE, OR KILLING FOLKS IN OUR HEARTS.

ALICE was the youngest of a large circle of brothers and sisters. She was the pet; but she was not a spoiled pet, willful and selfish, as pets are apt to be. She had a mother who made her children not only love, but revere and obey her. She was a praying mother, whose heart's desire, both by precept and example, was to lead her little ones to "the Lamb of God, which taketh away the sin of the world." The Holy Spirit owned this mother's efforts, and the four eldest were numbered among the people of God. Her first prayer for the little Alice was, that she might have an obedient heart and a tender conscience. Whenever she bathed her beautiful round limbs with pure water, she lifted up her soul to God, that her spirit might be cleansed with the pure river of the water of life, which proceedeth out of the throne of God and the Lamb. Alice was now five years old, and could you have seen her in company with her cousin Ruth, her playmate and schoolmate, as they dressed dolls or skipped off to school, you would have said, Surely innocence and love dwell in the bosom of these little ones.

One night when it was Alice's bedtime, she had no mind to go to bed. Sarah said, "Come, Alice, I will go up with you, for mother is engaged, you know." Alice sat still on the cricket,* looking down very sadly. She had scarcely tasted her bread and milk. "I am not a bit hungry," she said, shoving away the bowl.

"Do you feel sick?" asked Sarah.

"No, I am not sick," she answered. Again Sarah took her hand to lead her upstairs. "I wish mother would," said Alice; "I had a great deal rather mother would tonight." Sarah told her that her mother had company, and could not be spared; then she was led away, but slowly and unwillingly. As Sarah undressed her she

---

*Cricket—a low stool.

saw small tears flowing down her cheeks. "What is the matter, Alice? Tell me, child, what ails you," cried her sister anxiously. But Alice gave no reason, nor made a complaint, she only sighed. When it was time for her to kneel down by her little bed to pray, as her habit was, Alice knelt and bowed her head, but no words issued from her lips. Sarah thought this was strange. Then she arose and crept into bed so silent, so sad, so tearful, that Sarah became frightened. When she went downstairs and joined the company below, she watched an opportunity of mentioning the case to her mother. "I will run up directly and see what ails the child," said she. "Why, she is not sick, mother," said Sarah; "only it seems as if something was preying on her mind." Nor was it long before the mother escaped from the parlor and went to the chamber of her little one. As she trod the entry softly, lest Alice might then have fallen asleep, she listened and heard a low crying. "My child," said the mother tenderly, stooping down to her bedside, "what troubles you? tell me."

"Oh, mother, I am so glad you have come," cried Alice, un‐covering her head and seizing her mother's hand; "I can never go to sleep. Oh, mother, I *have killed* Ruth in *my heart* today; I did," and the tears flowed afresh. "She got angry, and I wished she was dead. I can't ask God's forgiveness till I've made up with Ruth. He won't hear me, for my heart had hatred in it, and not love, which displeases God. Oh, mother!" and the little child seemed broken in heart. Her mother tried to comfort her; but there lay the cold, heavy weight of sin upon her bosom. "Oh, if I could only see Ruth, and we could make up, then I could pray," she cried piteously. "Can't I go to Ruth's house?" The mother thought a moment, and then said, "Yes, my child, you shall go;" for she well knew no more important business could claim her attention than helping her child through the thorny passes of the "narrow way." Alice's father was called, who, wrapping the weeping Alice in a blanket, carried her to the home of cousin Ruth, whose door was next their own. She was taken to Ruth's bedside. It was a touching scene, the confession, the prayer for forgiveness, the kiss of reconciliation; then laying her head on her father's shoulder, she asked to be carried home. Once more in her chamber, Alice again knelt down and prayed God to forgive her for the sin of hating Ruth. "Give me love in my heart," she cried earnestly, "because God is love, and because it was love that made Jesus Christ die on the cross for us; give me love, for I want to be like Jesus Christ; keep me from hating and killing anybody in my heart." Thus prayed the little Alice. Oh, what a prayer and conflict was that. Sin and conscience, love and hatred had been fighting in her bosom. Alas, in the bosoms of how many children does hatred conquer love, does sin put out the light of conscience. In Alice love gained the mastery. Love to God, love to our fellows, love to do right, it is *this love* which makes us children of God; it is hatred and anger and strife which show us to be children of the devil. How many children who read this can remember hating and killing people in their hearts! Have you been sorry for it, and begged to be forgiven? If not, it shows you are far, far from God and holy things. Think of this.

GOOD AS OTHER FOLKS.

W HAT was your object in coming here tonight?" kindly asked a minister of a large boy who was present at an inquiry-meeting. "I came with Tom; he wanted me to come; he's my cousin," was the boy's answer. "You want to know how to become a better boy, I suppose," said the minister. "I don't know; I am about as good as other folks, I reckon," "That may be; but are you *good enough for God?*" The boy was silent.

After a little more talk, "I will put you in the way to ascertain how good you are; do you want to know?" asked the minister. "Yes, sir," answered the boy briskly. "When you go home, get paper and pencil, and write faithfully down all you do, your motives, your aims, your feelings, your thoughts, for the next three days; in a word, turn yourself inside out on the paper; write everything precisely as it is, for nobody to see but yourself; be honest about it, because nobody likes to deceive himself, you know: that will help you to calculate your goodness. Can you do that?" "Yes, sir," answered the boy, "I will."

When the meeting closed, Robert Greene left with different feelings from those with which he came. He came to get rid of his cousin's asking; and as he thought the minister would tell him how wicked he was, and talk to him about hell, he braced himself against any such attacks; "he was as good as other folks, he was sure." But when the minister put him in the way of reckoning up his goodness, the strange and unexpected turn of matters immediately interested him, and his prejudices against the meeting melted away. True, the minister talked just as he thought he would talk to some others, but not to *him*.

Robert took a sheet of paper that night and began his work. He had a strong box under his bed, and there he meant to hide it. As I said, he began that night. If anyone would like to see a part of this record, here it is:

"Tom asked me if I prayed before I went to bed. I don't. I never pray now. I never think of God at all. Morning. Got up as usual. Mother wanted me to split her some kindling wood to heat the oven; didn't want to; told her I had to go to school to do my sums; hooked my skates and went off skating till school-time: went to school; sums not done; copied them from Bill Poor's slate: master asked if we did them ourselves; made believe not hear him; tickled Bill in the class; he giggled, and master sent him to his seat; I sober as an owl: fired snowballs at an old drunken man; 't was real fun: asked father if I might go skating after school; father did not give me leave, so I gave him a dish of sulks; I sha'n't ask him next time. Father sent me down to squire Jones' office to get a paper; Jesse Jones and I got disput-ing; I mad; I swore at him; he said he'd tell my father; let him tell; I'll dare him to it."

So much for one day. When Robert went to bed he read it all over, once, twice, three times. The first thing in the morning he put his hand under the pillow, drew forth the paper, and read it while he lay in bed. "Here's deceit, selfishness, ugliness, and swearing," he might have said to himself, and I suppose he did. "This may be as good as other folks; but is it *good enough for God?*" What a solemn question had that grown to be. And although he knew his father, or his mother, or his minister, or Tom could never have guessed what was on that paper, and he was sure he would not have shown it to anybody for all the world, he could not help remembering that *God* searched him through and through. It was a very serious thought. It sobered Robert as he was never sobered before. "Good as other folks, but Oh, not good enough for God," he said again and again to himself. He did not believe he *was* as good as other folks. He thought nobody could show such a bad paper as his. He did not now need the minister to tell him what sin was. "And must I turn myself inside out two days more?" said Robert. Yes; he promised the minister he would.

The next week Robert was again at the inquiry-meeting. His manner was altogether changed. "Oh, sir," he said to the minister, "I am full of faults. I feel very wicked. God is angry with me. I am sure he will punish me. What shall I do to be saved?"

And here we leave Robert, trusting that as the Holy Spirit blessed the means used to discover his danger, the same Spirit will help him to find mercy and peace in Jesus Christ, the Redeemer of lost men.

This insensibility to our faults which makes people satisfied with being as good as other folks, you see is most dangerous ground. The word of God says there is "none good; no, not one." This is what makes your minister, your Sabbath-school teacher, and your pious parents so anxious about you. They know you are under the displeasure of God. They want you to feel your danger; for not until you feel it, will you seriously turn from your evil heart and go to the Lord Jesus Christ for mercy. He can change your heart, and give you that "holiness without which no man shall see the Lord."

CHRISTIAN CONSCIENCE.

I WANT to say something to the children about *Christian conscience*. What do you mean by *Christian conscience*? A conscience which takes alarm at little faults, and is afraid and ashamed of them because they are displeasing to God.

Jane had a new story-book, which one of her schoolmates came to borrow. "It's lent," said Jane; but when the child went away, her sister saw it upstairs. "That book is upstairs in your chamber," she told Jane. "You see, I didn't want to lend it to her," said Jane, "and I didn't want to hurt her feelings by a downright No; so I made that excuse." There are a great many such lies— good-natured lies—lies to save the feelings of others; and many people seem to think there can be no great harm in them.

The mischief is in thinking there is no great harm in sin except it happens to harm others, instead of regarding it as really committed against God, and displeasing to him. The lie of Ananias might have seemed harmless. It was told only to make Peter and his friends think better of him than he deserved. And yet God struck him dead; as if to show that such sins, however amiable or good they may make us appear, are in his sight sins of a deep dye. So Sapphira's lie was only told to screen her husband. And some one asks, Ought she not rather to shield than expose his faults? But what did Peter say? "How is it that you have agreed together to *tempt the Spirit of the Lord?* Behold, the feet of them that buried thy husband are at the door, and shall carry thee out." Here we may learn that God's judgment of what some call little sins is very different from ours.

There was a boy away at boarding-school. His father allowed him sufficient spending money, and told him never to have a bill at the stores. At the close of the half year he was in debt. "What will your friends say?" asked a class-mate. "Oh, there is no great harm done," he said; "father can very well afford to pay it." You see that the boy's notions of his fault relate only to the inconvenience it might or might not occasion to his parent; he probably did not think of it as anything which God regarded. But the boy's running in debt, small as it may have seemed to him, was an act of disobedience, a want of care over his heart and actions, a want of dutifulness towards God. It stands not as an injury done to his parents only, but to himself—an injury done to his good habits of watchfulness, of obedience, of acting so as to honor God. It stands therefore as a sin, and as such not to be forgotten before God, unless its guilt is washed out by the atoning blood of Christ.

How many words, actions, thoughts of our lives there are which give us no concern, and yet stand recorded as sins before God. What you need to cultivate, children, and what we all need to cultivate more and more, is a *Christian* conscience, which will not call evil good, which never excuses sins on account of their smallness, which never glosses over a fault because "no great harm" is done; but which sees in every sin a sin against the great and glorious Being who made you to be his holy and happy child.

The youngest person can understand that the death of the Son of God shows sin to be a very great evil. If God spared not his own Son, but freely gave him up for us all, it shows that what needed so great a remedy could never have been of small account; that when we commit a sin carelessly, and forget it, and never concern ourselves with it any more, we are making light of that which in God's sight is a sin so great that he gave his beloved Son to undo the mischief of it.

LUCY.

LUCY LIGHT was a dear little girl. She was a great favorite with her grandmamma, whom she visited every year; and grandmamma enjoyed her visits more than those of any other grandchild. Why? Because, instead of expecting her grandma to be always trying to entertain her, Lucy tried to please and interest grandma, and make her happy. There are children who think only of their own amusement, and never regard it a duty or a pleasure to sit down and comfort the lonely heart of the aged.

Lucy thought there was never a spot so pretty as her grand-mother's old garden door, and the rough old seats under the woodbine and honeysuckle. Here she used to fetch her Bible, and read and think; and the blue sky smiled, and the birds sang, and the flowers opened their bright eyes, and Lucy felt very happy. Was it the blue sky, or the birdies, or the flowers, which made her so happy? These certainly helped; but I do not think it was these alone. There was a little spring of peace bubbling up in her heart, which was, I think, the true secret of her happiness. What was it? The love of her Savior. Jesus' *love* was there, and it was a happiness nobody could take from her. The sky is sometimes clouded, birds cease their songs, friends may blame us or speak unkind words; but if Jesus' love is in the heart, there is always one sweet spot of peace and comfort left.

Lucy, when her lessons were over, often in school took her Bible and read. She loved the stories of Joseph, and Moses, and Samuel, and Queen Esther, and of Mary, and the child Jesus, more than any other stories. Her schoolmates used sometimes playfully to say, "Why, Lucy is 'Light,' and yet she is always trying to get more light." Yes, she was. How strange it is children should ever think religion made people dull and gloomy.

Piety is the greatest *cure* of gloominess or unhappiness, because it clears away selfishness from the heart. It puts kindness and forgiveness and love there. It lifts a ladder to heaven: prayer is that ladder; and holy desires and God's blessings are ascending and descending, like the angels on Jacob's ladder.

Pious people are very sorrowful sometimes, and grieve for the same reason Lucy did. Once Lucy's mother found her weeping sorely. "My child, what ails you?" she asked. Lucy did not tell at first; but seeing her mother looked distressed, she said, "Oh, mamma, because I have so much that is naughty in my heart. I want to be like Jesus." That was a cause for sorrow; but we may be sure, if any child grieves over secret sins in *that* way, she will never be satisfied till her sins are forgiven and washed away in her Savior's blood. Yes, and she will strive to be like Jesus—tender, forgiving, humble-minded, and full of good works.

THAT'S ENOUGH FOR ME.

❧

"WHAT do you do without a mother to tell all your troubles to?" asked a child who had a mother, of one who had not; her mother was dead.

"Mother told me whom to go to before she died," answered the little orphan; "I go to the Lord Jesus; he was my mother's friend, and he's mine."

"Jesus Christ is up in the sky; he is away off, and has a great many things to attend to in heaven. It is not likely he can stop to mind you."

"I do not know anything about that," said the orphan; "all I know is, *he says he will, and that's enough for me.*"

What a beautiful answer was that. And what was enough for this child, is enough for us all.

Are you tired of carrying about the heavy load of sin? "Come unto me, all ye that labor and are heavy-laden, and I will give you rest." But I am not worthy of his forgiving love. Never mind that. "He says he will, and that's enough for me." Take the Lord Jesus Christ at his word, for the forgiveness of your sins, and for peace to your soul. "My peace I give unto you," he says. Will he? Oh, his peace is very precious. Will he give us his peace? *"He says he will, and that's enough for me."* Trust him; his word never fails.

"Don't be frightened into religion," some say; "there is time enough yet to think of dying: besides, God is merciful; he will never cast the wicked down to hell."

Ah, you may do as you please, but as for me, I will take him at his word. *"He says he will, and that's enough for me."* God is angry with the wicked every day. "There is no peace, saith my God, to the wicked." Let me act accordingly, and flee from the wrath to come.

JOHN'S "BUT."

~

"I WANT to be a Christian, I want to repent and be forgiven, but"—so thought a lad when he saw the people of God more than ever in earnest to bring the young to a knowledge of the Savior. He felt that his mother prayed more for him. He read in the kind look of Mr. Mallen, his Sabbath-school teacher, "John, are you not going to choose *this* day what Master to serve?" "I wish I could," thought John, "I wish I could, with all my heart; *but*—" John felt the claims of a heavenly Master on his love and obedience, he *deeply* felt them; but—Oh, how many "buts" there are to hinder souls from meeting those claims; not that any "but" should weigh a feather in the great scale of heaven on one side, and hell on the other. Alas, they do. What was poor John's "but?"

John was fifteen; he well knew it was an important crisis in his character. Soon he was to leave home for a counting-room in a distant city. He wanted to enter it a Christian boy. It would be so much easier to *begin* so, than to change afterwards, for a Christian he must be some time. He could not for a moment bear the thought of dying unforgiven. Why not now resolve that as for *himself* he *would serve the Lord?* There was his *"but"* to hinder him.

One evening he went out to go to the chapel. He walked very fast. "Holloa," cried a boy, "stop;" and three boys ran down the steps of a house and followed him. "Where are you going in such a hurry?" they asked. "Got some business to attend to," said John. "Business?" cried one, laughing; "go with us." "Can't," said John. "You can," cried they.

"How shall I shake them off?" thought John anxiously. He passed the street in which the chapel stood. John looked down; he saw the lights, and the people going in. Why not tell the boys where he was going, and boldly leave them? He was afraid to. He was afraid they would laugh at him. So he walked on in their company until they reached a hall where some foolish exhibition was going on. "I've no money to spend here," said John, suddenly turning, and walking briskly away.

He nearly reached the chapel, when another group of the academy boys came along, and made a halt before the entrance. "What's going on here?" asked one. "Some meeting or other," answered another, "where they knock religion into people." It was bright moonlight. To avoid being seen, for you already perceive what John's difficulty was, he turned into a narrow passage leading behind the building. "Oh dear," he sighed in much distress, "this is the way I am losing the evening." He was indeed under the droppings of the sanctuary, but in a very odd place, where he would equally dread being caught by his pious friends or his irreligious companions. John felt mean. And what was worse, the boys sat down on the steps of the porch, and so he was prevented from making his escape at all. "If I could only hear," he thought, "and get a drop of good." But as it was, only the singing was of much account.

The next Sabbath his teacher was very tender in explaining the lesson to the class, and mingled more than usual personal instruction in it. John felt it, but he tried hard not to show his feelings. He wanted to feel inside, but not outside. He did not wish the class to see it. He turned round and looked another way. He tried to think of something that had made him angry, in order to brace his mind. Poor John. He went home feeling bad. "I want to be a Christian. I want to repent and be forgiven, *but*"—that was always the strain in which he spoke to his mother; and indeed her dear boy seemed near to the kingdom of heaven; why did he not enter in?

A day or two afterwards, on returning from the academy, he saw his minister on the doorstep, knocking. No one had come to the door. John ran along and asked him in: "Perhaps there's nobody at home, sir," said he. "I have come to see *you*, John," said the minister kindly. The boy's heart beat quick as with some awkwardness he led the way in and offered the gentleman a chair. Thu minister began to talk in his very kind way, and he drew, little by little, a great deal more out of John than he ever thought he could have told; yet it was far better that it should be so, in order that his minister might understand his difficulties and help him out of them.

"That *'but'* in your way, my young friend," he said, "is the *fear of the world;* almost everyone is surrounded by influences hostile to piety, and it *is* trying to encounter the cold, and perhaps scornful looks of some of your companions, which you are likely at first to do, in becoming a professed follower of Christ. 'The fear of man is a snare,' the Bible tells us. The Lord Jesus foretold all this; he stated very plainly what his followers might expect; he described the sacrifices they must make, and the trials they must endure for his sake. 'Whosoever he be of you, that forsaketh not *all* that he hath, cannot be my disciple.' How strongly is this expressed. What a full *giving up* of everything does he ask. And yet he says, 'My yoke is easy, and my burden is light.' One passage says it is hard, another that it is easy—the conditions of service appear to contradict themselves. How is this? It *is hard* to come to Jesus, because fear, pride, and many difficulties hedge up the way. But you must overcome them; and when this is done, when the trials are boldly met and the surrender once made and your heart yields to God, you will find the yoke easy and the burden light, and you will enjoy a peace and happiness which the world cannot give you, and which it cannot take from you."

When the minister left, he invited John to the chapel that evening. The boy thanked him, and promised to go; and "*I shall*," he said to himself; "God helping me, *I will*." When evening came, he wished his mother was going, but she was not well enough; and he set off alone. He secretly wished he might not meet any of the boys, but that trial had to be met; he had to make a distinct choice, *on his way to the chapel that night*, whom he would serve. The turning-points in people's lives are sometimes when they least expect them, and they often lie in a decision and choice concerning some seemingly small thing. In John's case he was abruptly brought to a turning-point.

"Where are you going, John?" asked Sam Kinsman, a hard sort of a boy, who had little respect for either God or man.

"To the prayer-meeting at the chapel," answered John.

"Going to have religion corked up in you?"

"*Yes, I am,*" answered John—and it seemed to him, as he said it, that a burden rolled from his back as it did from Pilgrim's. His step became lighter and freer.

The chapel was full. And when the hymn, "Not ashamed of Jesus," was sung, at the lines,

> "Ashamed of Jesus! That clear friend,
> On whom my hopes of heaven depend"—
> "Ashamed of Jesus! Yes, I may,
> When I've no guilt to wash away,"

John's heart melted, tears ran down his cheeks, and I don't think he would have cared then if the whole world saw him. John's *but* was all gone.

NO MIDDLE GROUND.

"FATHER, what do you think of Judge Sheppard? Don't you think he is a fine man?" asked Ashton Hall of his father. "He is an impartial judge on the bench," answered Mr. Hall; "he is what people call a good citizen, and a kind father." "And very good to the poor," added Ashton. "Very," said Mr. Hall. "And yet he is an infidel; he does not believe in the Bible, or prayer, or Sabbath-day, or any thing religious—you know he says he does not," said Ashton. "If we take him at his word, we must suppose he does not," said Mr. Hall. "Well, father," asked Ashton, "where do you think Judge Sheppard will go when he dies?"

"Why do you ask the question, my son?" "Why, father, because it seems as if there must be some middle ground between heaven and hell, where people only partly good and partly bad can go; right and wrong appear so mixed up in some people. How hard it seems to draw any line which will clearly put everybody on one side or the other. It puzzles me so," said the boy; "I've thought a good deal about it."

"The Bible settles your question, my son," said Mr. Hall. "You think the difference between the good and the bad is one of *degree*. You would ask how many more grains of goodness must one have to merit heaven, how many must one lose to lose heaven at last. Now the difference between the good and the bad in the eye of God, our eternal Judge, is not one of *degree* or *merit* at all. It is a difference in *nature* and in *title*."

"I do not understand you, sir," said Ashton, quickly. "In other words," continued his father, "the Bible, the word of God, tells us that the good are accepted not on account of any merit of their own; their only *title* to heaven is through the merits of Another. 'He that believeth on the *Son* hath everlasting life; and he that believeth not the Son shall not see life; but the wrath of

God abideth on him.' Another scripture says, 'He that hath the Son hath life; and he that hath not the Son hath not life.' Another says, 'He that believeth and is baptized shall be saved; but he that believeth not shall be damned.' Mark 16:16. You see it is only through an interest in the Son of God our Savior, that we have any title or door to heaven.

"The Bible also tell us that the *nature* which fits the good to enjoy heaven, is not the one which they have in common with all mankind, a nature which they were born with, but it is a nature formed within them *since* they were born. Turn to this scripture: 'Jesus answered, Verily, verily I say unto you, Except a man be born of water and of the Spirit, he cannot enter into the kingdom of God.' John 3:5. In Matthew you will find the Lord Jesus saying, 'Verily I say unto you, Except ye be converted, and become as little children, ye shall not enter into the kingdom of heaven.' Matt. 18:3. You see that the Scriptures are clear on this point. The Son of God is the way and the door to enter heaven by, which, if we refuse or neglect, no man can ever reach there. 'There is none other name under heaven given among men, whereby we must be saved,' the Bible again tells us."

"Then all our good qualities go for nothing," said Ashton. "They go for a great deal as far as they *do* go," said his father; "like the ornaments and conveniences of a house, giving it a very respectable look, and making it quite pleasant to live in, but offering no security against a rotten foundation. If that is not strong and safe, it will go to ruin, in spite of a good outside. The Scripture says, 'Other foundation' for our heavenly hopes 'can no man lay than *is* laid, Jesus Christ.'"

"Then how anxious we should be to bring people to Jesus Christ," exclaimed Ashton; "I never saw it just so before. Poor Judge Sheppard—can't somebody tell him?"

How many of the lovely, the amiable, the talented, those whom we love and respect, are there all around us, who, we fear, have never trusted their eternal interests in the keeping of the Son of God. Yet he says, *"I* am the way, and the truth, and the life: *no man cometh to the Father, but by me."* Oh, can't somebody tell them?

THE CHILDHOOD OF JESUS.

HOW much we should like to know about the childhood of the Son of God? Did he play and work like other boys? The Bible tells us but a few things about him. Why it does not tell us more, I do not know. It tells us that he "increased in wisdom." When he was twelve years old, he went to Jerusalem with his parents. On their journey home, they missed the boy. Where was he? Nobody had seen him. They hurried back to the city, and found him in the temple, "sitting in the midst of the doctors, hearing them, and asking them questions; and all that heard him were astonished at his understanding and his answers." He was never idle, never inattentive, never heedless; his whole mind and heart were open to receive instruction, and to impart it to others. How glad his parents were to find him, and among such wise and good people too. "Son, thy father and I have sought thee sorrowing," said his mother. "Did you not know," he said, "that I must be about my Father's business?" He was the Son of God, and God had sent him to this world to seek and to save them that were lost.

Jesus went home to Nazareth with his parents. And what was his conduct towards them? This is another thing the Bible tells us of his childhood: "He *was subject to them.*" He honored his parents. He was always obedient, always affectionate; he never spoke a cross word, was never unkind, never forgetful. He loved his Father in heaven, and loved the work which he gave him to do. He was a heavenly boy.

Do you not suppose the boys of Nazareth loved him dearly? But bad boys do not always love the good. They hate those whose spotless example reproves their wickedness.

The Son of God became a child that you may know how dear children are to him. He had a home just like you; he fulfilled all the duties of a child; he ate, and studied, and worked, and helped just like you. He remembers his childhood, and can feel for you. Whenever you think how you ought to behave, think of the heavenly boy that once lived in Nazareth, and how the Son of God, who became the son of man to save a wretched world, has set childhood a lovely pattern of early piety.

OUR WILLIE.

"OUR Willie has gone to the war," said the father with a manly pride that he had a son to give.

"Our Willie has gone to the war," said the mother in a low whisper, her heart almost breaking.

"Our Willie has gone to the war," cried Harry, wishing he had a soldier's sword too.

"Our Willie has gone to the war," said Mary, missing him so.

After Willie left, his room was kept just as he left it. On the shelf was a small brig, which he made and rigged when a little boy. Some book-shelves hung on the wall, his own handiwork also. Willie had a genius for such things. There were the books which he successively pored over, from Robert Dawson up to Cicero and Cambridge mathematics. On the table was the last book he read in the morning he left, "Lectures to Young Men," open to a chapter on "Responsibility." Irving's Life of Washington was near it, a book Willie had studied chapter after chapter, often affording a pleasant dish of talk with his father at meal-times.

Willie had graduated with respectable rank, and was on the point of entering his father's law-office when the war broke out. He was a youth of large promise, people said, sound at the core, the worthy son of most worthy parents. He was a child of prayer and of Christian nurture, and the mother kept hid in her heart the blades and shoots of his early piety, a sacred memory. As he grew to manhood he said less, but the roots were striking deeper, she hoped.

When the terrible rebellion came, Willie's soul was aglow. "Father, mother, shall *I* not go?" "Go, my son," said his father, the fire of patriotism burning out every other thought. Could mother say, "Go?" "God do with you as seemeth to him good, Willie," she said, her voice quivering under the strain of the costly sacrifice.

Willie went, and his home, like so many other homes, vibrated with the hopes and fears of a son and brother plunged into the perilous vicissitudes of war. The first thought in the morning and the last thought at night, in father and mother's bosom, was, "Willie, Willie." "Willie and the country" was the burden of their prayer. Willie and the country were one, garnered up in the agonizing supplication of how many souls!

Letters came every week. At first fresh with the novelties of a soldier's life, full of ardor and exultation. Then a more tender and earnest tone stole into the pages.

"Oh mother, forgive me all the sorrow and anxiety I have ever caused you and father. I feel that I have not been as good a son as I ought to have been."

"Dear parents, I feel your prayers around me. I am sure God will forgive and bless me for your sakes. War is pretty serious business."

"Dear father and mother, and Mary and Harry, if we should never meet here, I trust we shall be a united family in heaven. I try to make my parents' Savior my Savior. Make up your mind for the chances of war, father, and help mother too. But I hope for the best. This great and noble country is worth spilling one's blood for. I never for a moment was sorry I came, only I should like to see you all once more."

This was Willie's last letter but one. He was killed at the battle of Fair Oaks. Willie dead! God help his family. Oh, how many "Willies" are spilling their young, precious blood on the baffle-fields of the land, that our institutions, watered by hot blood and scalding tears, may be cleared of treachery, and rooted in righteousness and equal rights.

THE STING.

"MOTHER," said George, "when will Fanny come home? I wish you would write her to come."

"She went only yesterday, and will not be back these many weeks," answered the mother.

"Father, I wish you would write for Fanny to come back," said George at dinner-time.

"Grandmother will not be willing to spare her directly," father answered.

"How George hankers after Fanny," said mother to father; "he does not seem to care for the rest of us."

The children had a play-room, an open, unfinished chamber, where the boys had their gimblets,* saws, fishing-tackle, and nameless pieces of trumpery in one corner; and the girls occupied the opposite one with their babies and baby-house furniture of all sorts. It was about the sober gray of twilight, when, as the mother passed the door of the play-room, she heard a sound like crying, but it was a low cry. She stopped, and peeping into the room saw George sitting on a block whittling, with the tears running down his cheeks. She did not know whether to speak or not. Then, lest he might have cut him or be in pain, she asked, "What is the matter, my child?" George started, for he did not know anyone was by. "Nothing, nothing," he answered, wiping the tears from his face. "Where are James and Joseph?" asked his mother. "Gone in the wagon," answered George. "I did not want to go. Mother, do you think I shall ever see Fanny again? I sha'n't, I know." "I hope so," said the mother. "Why do you think you shall not?" George kept whittling, and the tears kept falling, falling, falling on the pine board and his knife.

---

*Gimblet—a tool for boring holes.

"I am glad you love Fanny so," said his mother, "and loving her so, I wonder you should wish to shorten her visit at dear grandmamma's, where the children have such nice times." George's tears only kept slowly falling, falling, and his mother looked on with pity; there was also a little surprise mixed with her pity, for she could not understand why George felt so much more than the other children. Fanny was a dear, good sister, but she and George had not seemed more necessary to each other's enjoyment than the others. After speaking a few cheerful words to her son, his mother left him, but she carried his sorrowful-face in her heart. At supper he looked brighter, and perhaps nobody but herself noticed the traces of his tears.

That night she sat up later than usual. On going to bed, "Mother, mother," came in a low whisper from the boy's chamber. The door was ajar; she pushed it open softly, and went in. George was wide awake; James and Joseph were asleep. George put his arms around his mother's neck and drew her to him, and she felt his cheek again wet with tears. "My dear boy," asked his mother tenderly, "what troubles you?" For a few moments his heart was too full to speak. "Oh, mother, I want to see Fanny so," he sobbed out on her bosom. "You love Fanny very much; do you not, George?" she said.

"Oh, mother, it is because I *hated* her. She came over in our play-corner the day before she went away, and I did not want her. I made up faces behind her back, and I would not speak to her; I was angry with her; I hated her; I wished she was off a thousand miles, and never would come back. Fanny don't know it, but *I* do, mother. I want her to come back; I want to see Fanny again, mother. Shall I ever see Fanny more?"

Poor George! A wounded conscience who can bear? Giving way to unkindness, anger, hate, towards those who love us, always leaves a sting behind, and that sting is called remorse. George was suffering from remorse. God has so made us, that sin, heart-sins as well as hand-sins, like stealing, or mouth-sins, like lying, bring their own punishment; just as goodness brings its own reward. Hating is a heart-sin. How many children have shed bitter tears in secret over the memory of hateful feelings against a father or mother, brothers or sisters, or some other friend who tenderly loved them? When these dear friends are away or dead, or you are removed from them, then how the thought of unkindness, felt or spoken, revives in the mind, biting like a serpent, and making our days very bitter. If we *could only* see them and make it all up by love and kindness again, we think— but this cannot always be done. Death may have snatched them away, and we cannot show kindness to the dead. "Get rid of such feelings the best way you can," said one boy to another, who was suffering from remorse for having treated his mother unkindly; "drown them, drown them." Yes, get rid of such feelings the best way you can, that is good advice; but do not try to drown them, that certainly will not remove the sting; but it is of great importance to know what will. Do not do any thing which will harden the heart more and more, and make it full of stings some day or other to be certainly felt.

What *is* the best way? I will tell you. Soften your remorse by *penitence*. Go and tell all to Jesus. Lay your burden at his feet. He is the friend and helper in such cases; and he will pour the balm of his *own love* into your poor wounded heart. We have not naturally love enough to prevent our gusts of ill-temper and evil feelings. We want more. We need to fill our hearts with love, that there be no room for hate. This is what the Lord Jesus can and will do for us. He will "shed abroad *his* love in our hearts;" and Oh, how full of kindness is his love. Did poor George get comforted so? I hope he did, for he was a very kind brother when I knew him.

A GOOD LION.

PATTY came to spend the day with her cousin Frank. They had nice plays together. "Now let us play Daniel in the lions' den," said Frank; "you be Daniel, and I'll throw you into the den, then I'll be the lions." "You won't eat me up," said Patty, in a little frightened voice. "No," said Frank; "you know Daniel wasn't eat up; he was too good to be eat, and the lions knew it. Besides, I shall only be a make-believe lion, you know."

Patty consented, so Frank put her into a dark hole behind the steps. Then he crawled in on his hands and knees, roaring and gnashing his teeth. Up he roared to Patty, and began to paw her, quite unlike the lions Daniel fell among. Such a specimen of the wild beast frightened poor Patty; and, dark as it was, she was not so sure that it was all make-believe. The little girl began to cry. Frank thought he must be playing lion admirably, and therefore roared and pawed the more, and got Patty's arm in his mouth, as if he were just ready to make a meal of her. Patty struggled to be free, and scrambling over a board, put up to fence the den off, she fell, and adding a hurt to her fright uttered a terrible scream.

When Frank found she was really crying, he jumped up, and throwing off the lion, "What's the matter, Patty?" he asked angrily. "I was afraid you'd turn lion and eat me up," sobbed Patty. "You little fool!" came up in his throat, but he did not say so; "you cry-baby!" he wanted to say, but did not. "You——" — he could have called Patty real hard names, but he promised his mother never to talk in that way. Frank was angry, and he was afraid he should say some naughty word. "I wish Jesus was here to help me do the thing that is right," thought the child, casting his eye up street. No Jesus was there, no *bodily* Jesus, at least; nobody you could see with your eyes. But Jesus *was* there truly. Frank knew that he was, and he suddenly shut his eyes tight up in order to see him. "Come, please, and help me, my God and Savior," he cried in his heart. Frank saw Jesus with the eye of faith; that is, he believed he was there to help him be a good boy, though he did not see him standing in the street.

Frank swallowed his angry feelings towards poor Patty, and a kind, pitying feeling took their place. He did not say she might have known better. He did not say it was not worth making such a fuss about. He did not say he would never play with such a little scare-crow again. He did not say it was all her own fault, and proudly leave her to have her cry out. That is what many boys would have done. And the little girl would have been very miserable, frightened, hurt, and Frank angry too, which would have made a heap of sorrow. No, Frank did not reproach her at all, or what would have been worse, *go off.* The Lord Jesus, whose help he invoked in this sad dilemma, taught him better. He taught him the sweet lesson of forbearance. "Patty," he said, going up to her, "I did not mean to frighten you. I played too rough. I'm sorry. We won't play lion any more; we'll play lamb or something else."

"I'm sorry too," sobbed the little girl, in a minute, as soon as she could speak; "but I could not help it. I was afraid you'd eat me up." "No, indeed," said Frank in a soothing tone, "I would not eat you up if I was a lion, Patty."

Comforted by this pleasing assurance, Patty wiped her eyes, and the two went away hand in hand, happy in each other.

"PLEASE, SIR."

"SIR, do you want to know how I was converted, I, an old grey-headed sinner?" said a good old man to a minister.

"Yes, tell me," answered the minister.

"I was walking along one day, and met a little boy. The little boy stopped at my side. 'Please, sir,' he said, 'will you take a tract? and please, sir, will you read it?' Tracts! I always hated tracts and such things, but that 'please, sir,' overcame me. I could not swear at that kind-spoken 'please, sir;' no, no. I took the tract, and I thanked the little boy, and I said I'd read it; and I did read it, and the reading of it saved my soul. I saw I was a sinner, and I saw that Jesus Christ could save me from my sins. That 'please, sir,' was the entering wedge to my old hickory heart."

THE LOST SHEEP.

THERE was once a Shepherd who had a hundred sheep. He led them "in green pastures and by still waters," guided them, and tenderly cared for every want. By and by one of his sheep strayed away, and was lost in the wilderness. Will the Shepherd go after this sheep and find it? He has ninety and nine safe in the fold. Has he not as many as he wants, and will he not let the poor wandering one perish? Ah no; he loves all his sheep. He will surely go forth and find it.

But does he not shrink to leave the pleasant fields and secure resting places where his dear sheep abide, to go into the wilderness, a dreary place, full of dangers and evils, hunger and pain and weariness? No; so great is his love for his sheep, so full of tender pity is his heart, that the good Shepherd will endure all this for the lost one. He leaves his flock and goes forth into the mountains and wilderness, and there patiently seeks to find the wanderer. It was a long search and a wearisome journey, for the sheep had strayed very far away. At last he finds it, sick and weary and hungry, for there had been none to care for it in the wilderness.

Does the Shepherd punish this foolish wandering sheep? Does he drive him roughly home? Oh, no. He binds up his wounds, speaks comforting words to him, lays him on his shoulder, and bears him gently and tenderly over the rough and thorny places of the wilderness till he reaches his own green pastures.

That sheep will surely cleave to his Deliverer. He knows what the wilderness is; he knows how sweet the peaceful fold of the Shepherd is. He knows too the dear love of the Shepherd as he never could have known it if he had not strayed and been brought home again. Oh how dearly for evermore he will love that Shepherd.

Who is this Shepherd? It is Christ. Who is the lost sheep? It is the sinner. Christ left the heavenly fold to find him. He is seeking for you, Oh lost one. Hear his voice, and go to him. He will not reproach or chide you, but gently lay you on his shoulder, and bear you home.

"Jesus my shepherd is;
'Twas he that loved my soul;
'Twas he that washed me in his blood;
'Twas he that made me whole;
'Twas he that sought the lost,
That found the wandering sheep;
'Twas he that brought me to the fold;
'Tis he that still doth keep."

THE LITTLE LAMB.

HOW green the pastures are! It is pleasanter to be out doors than in doors. "I almost want to be a real lamb now, to frisk on the soft hill-side all day long, or lie on the fresh grass, or lap from the cool spring brook."

There is a great deal in the Bible about sheep, and lambs, and shepherds. Jesus calls himself the Good Shepherd. Little children who love him are his lambs, and grown up people the sheep. Little children are called lambs because they are so gentle and playful, and easy to mind, and because they are so helpless and weak and tender, and apt to go where they will get harm.

"It does not seem as if we are good enough to be Jesus' lambs."

Do you suppose a good shepherd would say, I don't want any *playful* lambs in my flock? or any *foolish* ones that will be running away? or any *helpless* ones that I shall have to carry? No, no; no good shepherd ever says so. He knows lambs must frisk and play, and will be silly sometimes, and run away if he does not have his eye on them. That is lamb-life. And is not Jesus better than any shepherd that ever was? Do you think anyone ever heard him say, "That child is too playful to be in my fold?" Oh no. But he says, "That little boy is playful, and I must take him into my fold, where he will not find any thing hurtful to play with. That little girl does not know how to take care of herself; she shall come into my fold, and I will take care of her: when she is hungry I will feed her, and when she goes to sleep I will watch over her. And this naughty boy, who is so apt to run astray, may come back, and keep coming back, and I will receive and forgive him. And this poor wee lamb, so little and tender that it can't take one step, I will carry it in my bosom.

And this one that has got hurt among the rocks and thorns, I will take it in my arms. Let the children come unto me," he says, "and forbid them not; I died that they may live. 'Those that seek me early shall find me.'"

How good the Savior is! Yes. Try to keep by his side. You want to love him and please him, and yet every now and then you do foolish and naughty things, and stray off from his track. But do not run away from him. Keep running back to him, and he will love you, and watch over you. Try to be his little lambs. Oh, how blessed it is, that poor sinful, helpless, feeble little children have a Good Shepherd to go to, a Good Shepherd to love, to watch, to care for them, and a happy fold where the hungry wolves cannot get them.

POOR TOM.

I HAD been gone some weeks on a journey. Glancing over a newspaper issued in my absence, I met a paragraph which troubled me. It concerned a boy, one Tom Johnson, put in jail for robbing a gentleman's garden and barn. His accomplices escaped.

"Tom Johnson! Is that *our* Tom? Of course not." Yet I recollected not having seen him since my return. There was nobody near to inform me. "Tom," I kept saying; "it can't be *our* Tom. No, no." The next morning the first thing was to ask for Tom.

"Tom, our poor errand-boy? Hav'n't you heard? The poor fellow is in jail, and likely to go to prison. His trial comes on in the September term;" and the circumstances were rehearsed more at length than I found them in the paper. "Poor Tom," I could only say—it was a clear, sunshiny day—"Poor Tom caged up on such a bright day as this—he was as free as a bird, and yet I never thought him a vicious boy."

I determined to see him, and took the earliest opportunity of visiting him in his new quarters, and I am sorry to say it was the *first* visit I ever paid him. Pressing through the narrow, damp, foul-smelling gangway that led to his cell on the back side of the building, I felt sad enough. "A set of young rascals," said the turnkey; "pity the whole gang weren't here; and Tom Johnson's the ringleader of 'em."

"Yet I never saw any vicious leanings in the boy," I said. "Perhaps you don't know as well as you think for," said the turnkey. Perhaps I didn't, and so I did not stop to argue the point. When we reached the cell, whose door grated on its hinges as the man unlocked, opened it, and let me in, Tom was lying on his low cot, his head wrapped in the quilt. He started up, and rubbing his eyes, looked pleased when he saw who had come; then, as if suddenly recollecting where he was, his head dropped on his bosom, and he began to twirl the bedclothes with his fingers.

"Why, Tom, my boy, how are you?" I asked cheerfully. "So so," he answered, without looking up "I did not expect to find you here, Tom. How did it happen? How came you here?" "Oh, 'cause," answered Tom, "they put me in." I motioned the turn-key to leave us.

"Didn't you know 'twas wicked to steal, Tom?" said I, sitting down by his side. "Yes, sir; but didn't think much about that part of it." "Didn't you learn the ten commandments in Sabbath-school, Tom?" I asked. "Never went to Sabbath-school." "Never went to Sabbath-school? Why not, Tom?" "Nobody ever asked me to go." "Nobody ever asked you? Well, you ought to have gone, of course." "Didn't 'zactly know how," answered Tom. "When the Dow boys got their handsome paper, all pictured, I wished I could go, but nobody asked me." "Don't you go to meeting, Tom?" "No, sir." "Why, Tom, you ought to have gone to meeting, then you would never have come to this vile place." "My clothes wer'n't fit. The meetings you go to wouldn't have such folks as I be. Good many times I saw you go in, but was 'fraid to follow; they'd turned me out." "You've a mother, Tom, hav'n't you?" "No, sir; she's been dead ever since I gave up selling candy; had nobody to make it after she died." "Any father?" "No, sir; he's been dead always. I live with my cousins' folks; but they fight me." "Poor boy, why did you never tell me all this before?" "You never asked me," said Tom piteously.

When I first knew Tom, he used to come to the store with a clean box well stocked with molasses candy, and his clean and tidy appearance was a decided recommendation to his wares. There was a frank, prompt, respectful air about the boy which took my fancy, and he became our errand-boy. He did well for us, and we paid him well for his small services. But did our account *end* there? Did dollars and cents pay *all* I owed him? Ah, I began to be afraid not.

"I don't want to stay here," at length Tom said, bursting into tears; "it makes me sick. I feel awfully." "You see what comes of associating with such a set of fellows, Tom. They led you into evil courses." "Well, they liked me," said Tom sobbing, "and I didn't know much of anybody else since I went to my cousins'." "But you knew it was wicked, Tom." "Yes, sir; but it was meant more in sport than wickedness. We bet who was spryest." "Tell me how it happened." Tom told his story, a perfectly straight-forward one, I have no doubt, leaving a wide margin for those palliations of the wrong which the civil law cannot always fully recognize and allow. There was a pause. "Can't you get me clear, sir?" asked Tom. "I'll do what I can for you, my poor fellow." He squeezed my hand as I rose to go, and sobbed violently as I left him.

"The young rogue," said the turnkey, meeting me in the hall; "did you make much headway with him?" "I don't know," I said, and quickly left. How much I thought of poor Tom all the day through. Two or three spoke to me about him, and the *way* they spoke pained one exceedingly: "The little scamp," "The young rascal," and the free use of language whose harshness and heartlessness fairly startled me; and yet they were ordinarily accounted kind-hearted men. But they were ignorant, as I had been, of the state of society from which just such a class of boys naturally springs—an ignorance, however, which my conscience would not allow me to excuse. "The poor child," said Conscience; "*you* have helped make him what he is." I twinged. *I!* what had *I* done?

"You left *undone*—you did *nothing*," said Conscience. "You did not pay the debt of *moral* obligation which you owed him. God threw him in your way, a poor, friendless, uncared-for orphan; and if you did not know *who* or *what* he was, you *ought* to have known; you owed him a sympathy, a care, a helpful encourage-ment, which your superior situation imposed upon you. What might not your advice, your instructions, your warnings have saved him from? What might not your friendly interest in his sorrows and needs have made of him?"

The next day I went to see Tom again. I took an orange and a picture-book to him. "The boy is sick," said the turnkey, "and I really believe he is." "Well, Tom," I asked, sitting down by his side, "how are you?" "So so," he answered with a faint smile. I put the orange in his hand, and laid the little book on the coverlid. Oh, how I wanted to talk to Tom about his soul; but I did not know where or how to begin. Indeed it was awkward to begin *now* a friendly care for him, neglected all too long; for aught I knew, neglected till too late. And it was a bitter thought to me. While Tom was sucking his orange, I slipped out and borrowed a Bible of the jail-keeper. "Don't you want me to read to you, Tom?" "What's it about?" he asked. "You listen and see." I turned to the giving of the law on Mount Sinai, and read the account. "Big-thunderstorm, wasn't it?" said Tom, after I got through. I talked about the commandments, but he listened with very little interest. "Tom, you've read about Jesus Christ, and Judas who betrayed his Master? He was a thief, and you know what end he came to?" "What?" he asked. "He killed himself" "Killed himself? Perhaps he hadn't anybody to care for him" "Yes, he had; Jesus Christ cared for him."

Finding myself making small headway with the poor lad, I comforted myself with the hope of doing better next time. Tom grew sicker. The jail-keeper moved him to his own house, and I ordered everything to be done for his comfort. But it was his poor soul which weighed most heavily upon me. One day when we read to him the story of the cross, of Jesus Christ loving him and dying for *his* sins, tears ran down his cheeks. Tom's ear was gained, his heart was touched, and he listened to the prayer put up for him with serious and heartfelt attention. All exhortation and warning and instruction *short of this*, had failed of producing any strong impression upon the poor boy's conscience; this, the simple story of a dying Savior, moved and melted him as I had never seen him before. Then I felt hopes for Tom. "He will be a good man yet," I said to myself.

The next day his mind was wandering. A few more days and he was no more, and I followed him to the grave his chief mourner.

There is a large class of such boys as Tom to be *kindly* cared for. There are multitudes of boys and girls outside the church, outside the Sabbath, outside all religious and moral instruction, who may well say, "Nobody cares for my soul." Many a promising child is growing up in ignorance to be a blot upon society, a worse than useless citizen, a *lost one*, notwithstanding the death of Christ and his healing, who to all human view *might* be saved. Who is responsible? We must *seek them out*, as a man does his lost sheep or a woman her piece of silver. This is our proper Christian work. *We are responsible*. "To whom much is given, of him will much be required."

OUR FATHER'S CARE.

❧

"MOTHER, Mr. Green says he don't believe in providence. He says God don't mind us any more than we do the mites on a fig; and it seems likely, he has so many greater things to attend to. I don't see how he can."

The mother was busy then, and did not answer her boy. Ashton was sick and stayed at home that day, and he went roving about the house in quest of something to busy and interest himself about. Among other things he spied a new, warm overcoat in his chamber closet. "Oh, mother," he cried, running downstairs with it on, "is this mine? Where did it come from?" "Your father bought it for you," answered his mother. "'Tisn't weather for it yet," said Ashton, "but it will be soon. Father's always providing beforehand."

Ashton had scarcely finished admiring his coat when there was a knock at the door. He opened the door, and a man left an odd-looking chair. "Why, mother," cried Ashton, carrying it to her, "what in the world is this?" "A chair for poor lame Effie," said his mother; "how thankful she will be to get it." "I never saw one like it before." "I dare say not," said his mother; "your father planned it for Effie, and had it made. Let us carry it to her chamber." "I never saw any thing like father," cried the boy; "he can plan almost any thing." The chair was carried to Effie, and poor pale Effie was taken from the bed and laid in the little new chair. It had springs, and she could raise herself up and down, and wheel herself about almost anywhere. Altogether it was the nicest and queerest sort of chair he ever saw, Ashton said. As for Effie, she was as glad as could be.

The front door now opened, and children's voices were heard in the entry. "They've come," shouted Ashton: "I'm so glad." James, his brother of ten, and Mary, a little younger, bounded into the room, followed by a young man. "You like not to have seen us," cried James. "Such an escape!" echoed Mary. "Escape— from what?" asked the mother, looking towards the young man who came in with the children, and who was a law student in her husband's office. The long and short of the story was, that as James and Mary were coming from their grandmother's that morning, a three miles' walk, they found the little creek bridge in the Pines very rickety from the late freshet, and might have tumbled into the water in their attempts to cross it, had not the young man whom their father sent to meet them appeared just at that moment on the other side, and fixed the boards for them to cross in safety. "Father's always thinking of us," said James.

That night, when the mother went upstairs to see if Ashton was snugly in bed, "Oh, mother," he said, "wasn't it lucky father sent Mr. Jones for James and Mary? they'd surely been drowned. I know that bridge." "Father is always watchful, attentive, and foreseeing," said mother. "And never forgets," added Ashton, "and with all his law business to attend to. I don't see how he does it." "And yet you see that he does," said his mother. "In the first place, he provides us a house to live in, clothes to wear, food to eat, wood to burn. Besides this general superintendence for us all in common, he has a care suited to your different ages and wants—a *special* care for each of us." "That he has," exclaimed Ashton.

"Well, Ashton, if father with his large business can take such a general and particular care of his family, do you not suppose that God, the great Father of all, can and will take care of *his* great family? The superintending care which God exercises over all his creatures is called *providence*. He causes trees to grow, some for timber, some for fruit; grasses for cattle, and grain for men; night for sleep, and day for work. What he does for us all in common is called God's general providence. But his knowledge is as minute as it is vast; his care is as particular as it is universal. He hears the young ravens when they cry. Not a sparrow falls to the ground without his knowledge. He who sees and knows all things can have his eye on you and on the universe with as much ease as you can see me; and he has a care of people suited to their different wants. As a proof of his tender care, when we broke his laws and became subject to punishment, God *so loved* the world that he sent his beloved Son to seek and to save us. He died to forgive and bring you to heaven—*you*, my son."

Then the mother stopped speaking, kissed her boy, and left him thinking.

SOUND LOGIC.

"SIR," said a pious lad to his pastor one evening, "the fellows in our shop are always picking flaws in Christians, and arguing against the Bible, and I don't know how to answer them." "The best logic anyone can use," answered his pastor, "is the *logic of the life*. Give them that, and they can't gainsay you."

"The logic of the life?" asked the lad, not quite understanding what his pastor meant. "I will tell you," said he. "There was once employed at a dye-house as ungodly a set of fellows as could well be, scoffers at religion, despisers of the word of God, swearing, drinking, betting, fighting, gambling. At last one of the number was drawn to a prayer-meeting, when the Spirit of God laid hold of him. Poor John was almost in despair about his sins, which, he said, looked black and blacker. But Jesus Christ came and spoke peace to his soul. Light broke upon him. Old things passed away, and all things became new. John really was 'made over.' He gave up his cups and the companions of his cups. He brought home his wages, set up family prayer, and everything, both within and without, wore an altered and improved look. Two of his fellow-workers, seeing this change for the better, took to John's new ways, reformed, went to meeting with him, and behaved like good Christians. John joined the church, and from a tiger he became a lamb.

"John's religion was severely put to the proof at the dye-house. The dyers bantered him, ridiculed him, swore at him, and brought all their infidelity hotly to bear against both him and his religion. Tom and Jem tried for a time to stand up for him, and withstand the ungodly storm of their persecuting associates; but after a while they *gave in*, grew ashamed of their religion, deserted John, and went back to their old ways. As for John, much as his temper was tried, he bore himself patiently, watched over his weak points, clung closer to Christ, and stood firm as a rock. Poor John never undertook to *say* much; but his consistent Christian life was a powerful plea in behalf of his principles. One day, however, after his fellow-workmen had been boasting what good infidelity would do, and how much harm the Bible had done, John's soul was stirred within him; he turned round, and said feelingly, but firmly, 'Well, let us deal plainly in this matter, my friends, and judge of the tree by the fruit it bears. You call yourselves infidels. Let us see what your principles do. I suppose what they do on a small scale they will do on a large one. Now there are Tom and Jem,' pointing to the two who went with him and then turned back. 'You have tried your principles on them, and know what they have done for them. When they tried to serve Christ, they were civil, good-tempered, kind husbands and fathers. They were cheerful, hard-working, and ready to oblige. What have you made them? Look and see. They are cast down and cross; their months are full of cursing and filthiness; they are drunk every week, their children half clothed, their wives broken-hearted, their homes wretched. That is what your principles have done.

"'Now I have tried Christ and his religion; and what has it done for me? You know well what I used to be. There were none of you that could drink so much, swear so desperately, and fight so masterly. I had no money, and nobody would trust me. My wife was ill-used. I was ill-humored, hateful, and hating. What has religion done for me? Thank God, I am not afraid to put it to you. Am I not a happier man than I was? Am I not a better workman and a kinder companion? Would I once have put up with what I now bear from you? I could beat any of you as easily now as ever. Why don't I? Do you hear a foul word from my mouth? Do you catch me at a public-house?* Has anybody a score against me? Go and ask my neighbors if I am not altered for the better. Go and ask my wife. Let my house bear witness. God be praised, here is what Christianity has done for me; there is what infidelity has done for Jem and Tom.'

---

*Public-house—a pub or drinking establishment.

"John stopped. The dyers had not a word to say. He used a logic they could not answer, the *logic of life*. If you cannot *argue*, you can *act*. If you cannot reason with the enemies of the Bible, you can live out its blessed truths, and so 'with *well-doing* put to silence the ignorance of foolish men.'"

OLD PETER.

PETER was an old sailor. A vessel in which he once shipped was struck by lightning, and one of his shipmates was killed. This sobered Peter. It made him think, he said, of the judgment-day. He went to his locker, and took out his Bible. "I want to find the Pilot that can weather me through that storm," said Peter; "it's scary business, shipmates, to find us on a lee-shore there, with the rocks of our sins right 'longside, and hell yawning not far off."

Peter took to his Bible. He did not make much headway until he came into port, and went straight to a Bethel, or sailor's church, which he did as soon as he was off duty.

"I want to find the good Pilot," said Peter to the minister after service.

"The great Captain of your salvation, Jesus Christ," said the minister; "he's here. He's nigh to every poor sinner that calls upon him."

"I'm one on 'em," said Peter, the tears streaming down his sunburnt cheeks, "and I want to ship in his service. I am pretty near waterlogged in my sins; I ha'n't any chart, compass, or anchor, and I'm drifting to perdition. I want the Pilot that went to the fishing-smack* on Galilee, and said to the skipper when he was well-nigh sinking, 'It is I; be not afraid.' How shall I get at him?"

"Down on your knees, Peter, and pray; tell him just how you feel, and just what you want, and don't give up or put off till you find him: for he says himself, 'Ask, and you shall receive; seek, and you shall find.'"

Peter and the minister knelt down to pray in the Bethel, for the people had gone, and Peter cried mightily unto the Lord.

---

*Smack—a small boat.

"Save me, Lord, or I perish," was the burden of his prayer.

And the next time his shipmates saw Peter, he really seemed a "new man." Some people say you cannot get religion in a minute; but the fact is, it does not take God long to pardon your sins, if you only are honestly setting out to get them pardoned. It does not take long for a man to tack about, when he once sees he is on the tack of ruin. "Right about" from a bad road to a good road may be done as fast as steps can carry you; but it can't be done without the *first* step, and that is really the decisive, the most important step of all. "Turn, sinner, turn." "Ye shall seek me and find me, when ye shall search for me with all your heart." And God will forgive a poor sinner, and receive him to favor, and make him one of his people, just as soon as he does this. So that "getting religion," as some people call it, or being saved from the dreadful consequences of your sins by the blood of Jesus Christ, who died "the just for the unjust," may be, and really is a very short work; it is a simple act on your part—a childlike giving up of yourself to God. This is what the penitent thief on the cross did; and he had time to do no more. Building up a religious character indeed takes time; it is the growth of months and years.

Well, from that time Peter was "a new man." People saw that he was indeed the old weather-beaten tar he was before, but a changed spirit was in the man. Instead of the swearing, drinking, reckless, spending old Peter, he was clean-mouthed, sober, humble, anxious to have everybody else ship in the same service he had.

"Don't put it off," he used to say. Testament in hand, he is talking to an old sailor. "I must take time to think of it," says he. "To think of what?" cried old Peter; "whether you are a sinner? You know you are. Whether you'll be lost if you die as you are? You know you will. Whether the Lord Jesus can save you? You know he can. Breakers are ahead. Your anchors won't hold you. *Don't put it off.*"

"I am not so bad as you think; I am not so bad as others," says another.

"But you are bad enough," cries old Peter. "The best sinner on earth is too bad for heaven. One sin ruined Adam. You are drifting, God knows where. This calm is dreadful. Your keel will soon ground on the rocks. Would that you would cry out now, 'God be merciful to me a sinner!' A storm is brewing. Hail the great Pilot. Don't put it off."

Old Peter loved the young people. "Bless God that you are young," he used to say. "'They that seek me *early* shall find me.' The great Captain of our salvation loves the young. Ship in his service, boys. 'Remember *now* thy Creator in the days of thy youth, while the evil days come not.' Then your rudder never'll snap; you'll never drag your anchors; the devil's craft will never run into you. Ship in His service, boys, and *don't put it off.*"

GOOD RESOLUTIONS.

JESSIE came home from school, and seeing the closet door open, she went in. In one corner of the closet stood a jar, where her mother usually kept Bath-biscuit—a nice rich cake which Jessie was very fond of. She opened the jar, and looked in, and put in her hand and took a couple out. Hearing a sudden noise while in the act, she started like a guilty person, and wanted to hide. However, she took two, hastily ate one, slipped the other in her pocket, and ran out-doors. After both were eaten, and the pleasure gone, Jessie felt very ill at ease. She wished she had not taken them. She shrank from appearing at the tea-table, lest her mother should have found that two cakes were missing, and might suspect *her*. You see how very suspicious guilt is.

"I will never, *never* do so again," said Jessie to herself that night. "I'll always ask. It is a sort of stealing to take things so; it is sin. I'll never do so again; and so I've said before, over and over," thought the child, as a miserable sense of broken resolutions crossed her mind. "Oh dear," she groaned, "I want to be good, but I can't." She tried to pray, and after a great while went to sleep, with a "never do so again" on her lips and in her heart.

The next day, at recess, Martha Scott called a few of her cronies to her desk. "See here, girls, what I have got." They huddled round, when she opened a paper, and displayed six large pickles, for some school-girls have an unaccountable liking for pickles. The girls set up a shout. "Did your mother give them to you?" asked one. "Of course she didn't," answered Martha. "It's wrong to take without leave," said Jessie. "I guess Jessie's conscience isn't clear on that point," cried one of the girls sharply. "Well, it's wrong," persisted Jessie. "Do *you* always ask leave?" "Come now, Jessie, do you? Miss Reproof, do you?" cried

Martha Scott. "Yes," cried Jessie, quickly and angrily, "I do." She certainly spoke before she thought. "Jessie, Jessie," whispered conscience, "that is a lie." "I know it, I know it," whispered Jessie back, in anguish of spirit. Jessie helped eat the pickles; but something stuck in her throat. It was not the pickle; I think it was the lie.

"Oh dear, dear," she said to herself, and all day it was inside, "Oh dear, dear;" which meant, "What a weak, sinful thing I am; I can't keep my resolutions. When I am tempted, they are like cobwebs before aunty's dust-brush; 'tis no use to make them. I shall never be good, never, never."

As soon as Jessie had an opportunity, which was the next day, she asked, "Do you think, mother, it is of any use to make good resolutions? Do you think they make us any better?" She wanted very much to understand the matter, for Jessie had had the notion that good resolutions had a great deal to do with making people good. Her own experience had indeed been quite to the contrary, and what it all meant puzzled her sorely. Therefore she anxiously waited for her mother's answer. "Not when good resolutions take the place of something *to be done*; not when they take the place of penitence," answered her mother; "for there are some people who ease their conscience by good resolutions against sin and temptation *to come*, when they should be repenting and giving up that sin which made their conscience ill at ease." "How repent, and give it up?" asked Jessie. "Be so truly and thoroughly sorry for it, as to be willing to confess it, to feel very humble on account of it, and to desire above all things to be separated from it—to be 'washed from it,' as the Bible says." "And how *can* we feel so?" asked Jessie with tender concern. "By the help of the Holy Spirit," answered her mother; "that is his work: to *convince* us of sin; to mellow our hearts, and make us ready and willing to give up thoroughly everything which grieves and displeases God."

" 'Holy Spirit'—I never thought of that before; '*confess* it'—I never thought of that before," said Jessie, only half aloud, as if speaking to herself; she looked very serious: "and resolutions, mamma—" But mamma was gone. The baby was crying in the distance.

Jessie went away full of new ideas. She had heard the same things over and over, I dare say; but now they made an impression, because she felt she had a personal interest in them as she never had before. That night, as Jessie's mother sat alone reading in the sitting-room, and the children had long ago gone to bed, the door opened gently, and, "Mother, are you alone?" came softly through the little crack. "Jessie," exclaimed her mother, holding out her hand; "come in, child. What is the matter?" Jessie stole in, and taking her mother's stretched-out hand, and resting her head on her mother's shoulder, she sobbed out, "Oh, mother—" Then what did she do? She confessed taking the Bath-biscuit, the weakness of her good resolutions, the next-day lie, and all the wretchedness which followed. Penitent and humble, she sank at her mother's knee, not to "*say her prayers*," that is, use words upon a thoughtless tongue, as she had done so often before; but she prayed, "O God, forgive me, for Jesus' sake."

And did Jessie ever confess to Martha Scott the lie she told her? Yes, for she meant to make a clean breast of it. And what did Martha Scott say, do you suppose? "You foolish girl, Jessie," she cried. "I'd never confess I told a lie till doomsday; you are a foolish girl." If her mother's tender and approving looks had spoken peace to her troubled soul, Martha's hard and unfeeling words stung her to the quick. Jessie had yet to learn how differently the people of the world view the feelings of the penitent heart from God's people. The people of the world hug sin, and are too proud to give it up; while there is joy in the pious heart, yes, and *joy in heaven* over one sinner that repenteth.

Children who are taking the first steps in a heavenly life, must not be frightened and discouraged by such harsh treatment from their mates; they will find a sweetness and love in their own bosoms which more than make up for every unkindness; and this is to be got, not merely by making good resolutions against the future inroads of sin, which I think is all that many do who are disappointed at finding no real comfort and strength in it, but by a penitent confession, a thorough *now* giving up of what is wrong—not of one fault only, but all your faults; not repenting for a fault once, but every time it over-comes or tempts you. Take a bad act in hand *at once*, like a fever, or any other dangerous disease. How odd it would be if a person sick of fever should lay groaning to himself, "I resolve never, never to have another fever," without taking proper measures to get rid of the one he already has, and eradicating it from his system. It is *curing* he wants, and good resolutions are not medicine; but they are excellent to strengthen and brace the body after it is cured.

SHOWING HIS COLORS.

❧

ONE of the noblest and bravest of the young English officers who perished in the Crimean war was Captain Hedley Vicars. We are apt to think that a soldier's life is inconsistent with piety; but he united the service of his heavenly Master with service to his country.

While stationed at Halifax, in the year 1851, he one day, in waiting for a brother officer, idly turned over the leaves of a Bible which lay on the table. The words caught his eye, "The blood of Jesus Christ his Son cleanseth us from all sin." Shutting the book, he said, "If this be true for me, henceforth I will live, by the grace of God, as a man should live who has been washed in the blood of Jesus Christ."

That night be scarcely slept. It was passed in solemn thought and in prayer. The next morning he said, "The past then is blotted out. What I have to do is to go forward. I cannot return to the sins from which my Savior has cleansed me with his own blood." The first thing he did was to buy a large Bible, and place it open on the table in his sitting-room, determined that "an open Bible" for the future should be "his colors." "It must speak for me," he said, "before I am strong enough to speak for myself." His friends came as usual to his rooms, but they did not fancy his new colors. They laughed at him for "turning Methodist;" and for a time his quarters were quite deserted. Did that frighten him? No. It was hard work to stand his ground, he said; but the promise did not fail, that "the righteous shall hold on his way, and he that hath clean hands shall wax stronger and stronger." Henceforth the word of God was the "man of his counsel," and he set apart no less than three hours each day for the study of the Bible and prayer. At one time he wrote to his sister, "I generally spend four or five hours each day, when not on duty, in reading the Bible and meditation and prayer."

"Everyone loved and respected Vicars," said a fellow-officer after his death at the age of twenty-eight. "Those who did not agree with his strict religion, and those who used to know him as the leader of many a mad riot, closely watching him for years after he enlisted in Christ's army, at last gave in, and declared he *never flinched;* that whoever else was not, he was in very truth a *whole Christian.*"

This is the highest thing which can be said of a man. Now what is it that makes a *whole* Christian? He *feeds* upon Bible truth. He gives *hours* to the study of God's word, and not a few minutes, which too many people are content to give to the Bible. It is divine truth which makes the soul grow. This is the living bread which nourishes and ripens a man's piety. You see what a prominence this young officer gave to Bible reading. He did not shove it aside for other reading, but made his Bible first and foremost among all other books or business.

There are a great many young people, boys and girls, all over the country, just entering upon the Christian life. If you would have your piety worth anything to yourself, *study your Bible.* If you would have your piety worth anything to others, *study your Bible.* If you would become a "bright and shining light" in the world, or be in any measure a useful Christian, feed your soul with the word of God.

THE BEST FIGHT.

THE boys in our neighborhood formed a company. They called it the State Guards. They had uniforms and banners, and a drum and fife, and looked quite military. They were of all sizes, little boys and big boys. The big boys did not want the little boys, but the little boys *would*. Their march through the street attracted a good deal of attention, and a posse of idlers ran after them as they run after soldiers of a larger growth.

"I wish we had somebody to fight," said the captain. "I should like no better fun than to go to battle and kill somebody."

"What a pity there is so much fight in us," said a timid mother.

Pity! Oh no. I am glad there is, for there is a great deal of fighting to do. The only concern is, that the boys should get into the best fight.

"Best fight! I did not know there was any best to it. I thought all fighting was bad."

Yes, there is. Do you want to know what it is. *"Overcome evil with good."* Overcome means to get the best of, to conquer. This warfare is the best warfare; it has several advantages.

It is the *cheapest* kind. War, you know, costs a great deal. The equipments of a new military company formed here not long ago, cost each man, to begin with, one hundred and twenty dollars. If it goes into battle, the expense will be vastly increased. Different assessments will be made on different men. Some it will cost an arm, some an eye, some a lip; to some, life itself. Our Revolutionary War cost fifty million dollars a year, and it lasted seven years. How much did that come to? A round sum. And it cost England twice as much. But to "overcome evil with good" no powder or shot is necessary—no Sharpe's rifles or Colt's revolvers. The sole ammunition is kindness; the only charge is love.

Another advantage is, that it is *safer*. War is full of danger and privation, and sickness and death. Did you ever read a description of a battle-field—surgeons at work from morning till night, ready to faint with fatigue, and scores of poor soldiers begging for their turn to come next? But in the "best fight" no limbs are shot off; no blood is shed; no lives are taken; no children made orphans, no wives made widows. It is safe, and pleasant as safe, and safe as pleasant.

Another advantage of this fighting over all other kinds is, that it is *surer to beat*. There was once a cross woman who lived in an old house alone. Nobody *could* live with her. She was called a *virago*.* The neighbors had as little to do with her as possible. The children were dreadfully afraid of her. A new family from the country moved into the next house, and the good woman was not slow in learning the character of "Ma'am Bates." "She'll kill your hens, stone your kitten, and do everything to plague you." "Oh, never mind," said Mrs. Gray, "if she does; I shall contrive to *kill her*." What, had the neighborhood got another edition of Ma'am Bates? Could pleasant-spoken Mrs. Gray *kill* anybody? Well, it was not long before she had a touch of "Ma'am Bates'" tongue, and it was enough to cut you in two. So when Mrs. Gray had a barrel of nice apples from the country, she sent a basketful in to her; that was *her* way of fighting; but never a word of thanks did the little girl get who fetched them. Instead of thanking her, what should the ugly old creature do but toss them all over into Mrs. Gray's back yard, most of them into the mud. That was not all. Mrs. Gray had a little dog Fido, who, just as he used to do in the country, made friendly calls in the neighboring yards. Fido certainly meant no harm. One day, finding Ma'am Bates' gate open, in an evil moment the little dog trotted in. And what should she do but pour a ladle of hot suds on his back. Poor Fido ran yelping home, and it was a long time before he got well of his scald. What did Mrs. Gray do? Did she scald Ma'am Bates' black cat? No, no. The old woman had a troublesome cough, and Mrs. Gray

---

*Virago—a strong, bold woman.

carried her in some medicine for it.

Mrs. Gray, not many weeks after, while washing at her back
door, heard low groans. She listened. "Something has happened
to poor Ma'am Bates," said the little woman, leaving her tub
and going round to see what the matter was. Sure enough, the
old creature had fallen down with an armful of wood, and so
turned her ankle that she could not get up. Mrs. Gray hoisted
her up as well as she could, helped her into the house, bathed
her ankle in linament, put her in bed, and brought her some
warm tea from her own teapot. "Oh," cried Ma'am Bates, the

tears rolling down her weather-beaten cheeks in spite of herself, "neighbor, you'll fairly *kill* me with kindness." "That's just what I *mean* to do," said the good little woman.

Well, she *was* killed. The *virago* was killed; and when Ma'am Bates got out again, she proved to be as good a neighbor as anybody. The police could not make her. Bridewell could not, for she had been locked up there. Retaliation could not do it; that is, treating *her* as she treated others; it made her worse. The tit-for-tat policy is a poor one. Mrs. Gray fought on surer ground; she "overcame evil with good." Kindness conquered. Love made sure work of it. The old woman could foil every other weapon; but kindness she couldn't. Nobody can stand its fire long without giving up.

Should you not like to enlist in the company who fight with such weapons? Jesus Christ is Captain of it. Love is the uniform. It is an "army with banners." Here are some of the mottoes: "A kiss for a blow;" "Conquer by kindness;" "Overcome evil with good." And the best of it is, all the children can join; none too young, or too poorly educated, or too feeble-minded. They may all fight this fight, and come off conquerors, and more than conquerors, through him that loved us, Jesus Christ; who *so* loved us that he came to this world filled with enemies to redeem us from sin and help us in this best of fights, "overcoming evil with good."

WHY THE BIBLE DON'T TELL MORE.

"WHY don't the Bible tell about *more* things, mother? It might, God knows so much." "What books are those on the lower shelves of the library?" asked she. "The large ones there are so many of?" asked Henry. Henry went towards them, and read, "En-cy-clo-pe-dia," a long hard word; "What does it mean?" he asked.

"A collection of the principal facts and discoveries in the different branches of knowledge," answered his mother. "There is something about medicine, and steam-engines, and water-wheels, and coal, and china, and almost everything you can think of."

"How many volumes there are," said Henry; "I'll count them—one, two, three, four;" and so he counted on to thirty. "Thirty big volumes. I should think it would take a life as long as grandpa's to master them."

"One person is not likely to be interested in every subject that is treated of," said his mother. "One might wish to learn about spinning, another mining, another about beehives. That would depend upon people's taste and studies. Caroline, you know, was hunting the other day for the camel."

"It is strange *I* have never been to them since I have been at Uncle Henry's," said the boy: "but, mother, didn't they cost a great deal?"

"Perhaps about five dollars a volume."

"Five dollars a volume, and thirty volumes; that would be one hundred and fifty dollars," cried Henry. "It's not many who could afford to buy them."

"You now see why the Bible is not an encyclopedia, telling about a great many more things than it does. It would then have told many things interesting to some people, and having no interest to others. The Bible only tells what is important for all men—for all men, women, and children to know; for in some respects they are all upon the same footing. What does the Bible teach?"

"The creation of the world, and when the Sabbath was made; about Adam and Eve, and how they sinned; about God's giving his law on Mount Sinai; about Jesus Christ our Savior; about heaven and hell, and all such things," answered Henry.

"Just such things as are of common concern to us all," said his mother. "It is of no importance for me to understand how the great wheel of the factory turns all the little wheels, but it is for Mr. Miles the engineer. Neither does it concern him how to cut a man's leg off in the most skillful manner; that belongs to surgery, and Uncle Henry knows about that because he is a surgeon. Uncle Henry and Mr. Miles therefore need to study different things, in order to be skillful in their different branches of business. They are not on common ground there, you see. But it concerns equally Mr. Miles, Uncle Henry, and you and me to know there is a hell for the wicked and a heaven for the right-eous, that we are sinners, and that God has provided a way to escape the consequences of our sins. Why are these more impor-tant to know, and equally important for us all, Henry?"

"Because these are about eternal things, for ever important," answered Henry. "Eternity is millions longer than time."

"The Bible then teaches what is most important for every-body to know, and which could not have been known unless God told it, and it is silent about everything else."

"Now I see why the Bible should be what my teacher calls it, *much in little;*' it is so important, that it is made little to carry about and easy to remember. Oh how hard to carry about, either in your head or your hand, thirty volumes of the Encyclopedia."

"And cheap enough for the poorest person," added his mother. "Ten cents will buy a Testament, which contains more knowl-edge valuable to us than all other knowledge put together."

"Only think, mother, neither I nor any of us children ever

looked into Uncle Henry's En-cy-clo-pe-dia, but we read the Bible every day, and I can carry my pocket Testament in the smallest pocket I've got. Yes, mother, I can carry all God's written law in my own pocket, when the laws of our state, Oh how many shelves they covered: Uncle Henry showed us in the State-house."

"God's laws are all comprised in two," said his mother. "Do you know what they are, Henry?"

"Thou shalt love the Lord thy God with all thy heart, and with all thy mind, and with all thy strength; and thy neighbor as thyself."

THE YOUNG MISSIONARY.

DAVID was the name of a little boy born in Haddam, Connecticut, many years ago. He was the third child of a large family of brothers and sisters, whose parents both died before David was fourteen. The family were then scattered. It is a sad thing to be an orphan, and grow up without a father's care or mother's love. But God took care of David, and adopted him into *his* happy family.

When only eight years old, this little boy began to seek after God. He did not at first find him. He did not quite know the way, and therefore it often looked dark, and he was greatly troubled: but God had sent his Son to be the little boy's Savior, and the Holy Spirit to make him humble and willing to follow him. How happy was David when he found God. He loved to go out into the woods and praise and pray to him; and sometimes the trees and grass seemed to *shine* with God's love.

David worked on a farm. As he grew older, he wanted to go to college and become a preacher of the gospel. His friends were willing he should, and he entered Yale college, at New Haven. After staying three years, poor David was expelled. What, did he become bad? you ask. No, no. In his room one day he said some hasty thing about one of the officers of the college, which an ill-natured person reported. It gave great offence, and was the occasion of his leaving college; but it left no serious blot upon his character. Still it was a great trial to David, and drew him closer and closer to his heavenly Friend. "Oh," he said, *"one hour with God* infinitely exceeds all other delights and pleasures."

There were a great many Indians at that time all around the white settlements. Western New York was all forest and red men. The western part of Pennsylvania also was a wilderness, filled with Indian tribes, for as yet none of the western states were born. The poor Indians were "without God in the world," and David pitied their lost and wretched condition. "Without God!" The young man knew how delightful it was to be *with* God, and he could conceive how awful it must be to be without him. He longed to go and tell them of the good God who made them, and sent his Son to redeem them from their sins and lead poor sinners into heavenly ways.

This desire in his heart soon found an outlet. A missionary society in England wanted to send the gospel to the savages, for there was no such society in this country then, and it sent word to some ministers in New York to choose a young man to go. They immediately chose David Brainerd. "Will you go," they asked, "and tell the poor Indians about Jesus Christ?" When the offer was made, he went away with two or three Christian friends and prayed; "and indeed it was a sweet season to me," he said. Then he answered, "Yes, I will go;" and so he became a missionary, and made his preparations accordingly.

He must have an *interpreter*, for he could not speak Indian; and an intelligent young Indian was found named John Wau-waumpequunnaunt. There were no roads through the immense forests, and they had to make their way as best they could, on horseback, over high mountains, through deep valleys, fording streams, and cutting their way through woods howling with wild beasts. In travelling from village to village, and wigwam to wigwam, sometimes they lost their course, and were overtaken by furious storms. A bundle of straw was the young man's bed; boiled corn and hasty pudding his chief food. And so he went and preached all about the forks of the Delaware and Susquehanna rivers, in danger, in sickness, and in want often. But his labor was not in vain. God wonderfully blessed the preaching of the white man to the poor red man, and many, many turned from their wicked heathen ways to Christ. Sometimes whole companies melted into tears at the sweet story of the Son of God, and would cry out, each one for himself, "Guttummau-kalummeh; guttummaukalummeh—Have mercy on me; have

mercy on me." "Wechaumeh kmeleh Nolah; wechaumeh kmeleh Nolah—Give me a new heart; give me a new heart." A great many found the dear and precious Savior. "Me heart glad," they said. "Jesus Christ do what he please with me." "How can me live in this wicked world? Me 'fraid sin more. Oh, dear Jesus, let me come to you." Numbers professed Christ, and led happy Christian lives.

The young missionary spent two years on this field. When he went to it there was no voice of prayer, no tear of penitence, over all this wild heathen wilderness. When he left, it was

dotted with the sweet blossoms of pious hopes, and almost
every wigwam was a place of prayer.

At the end of two years David left, and visited the white settlements to recruit his failing health. He visited Boston and
stopped in Northampton at the house of President Edwards,
where he died at the early age of twenty-nine. "My heart is
sweetly set on God," he said. "I long to be with him, and see his
glory." This was in the fall of 1747, more than a hundred years
ago. Proud men at the time might have said, "What a waste of
life; the young man has not lived to do anything." And I have
brought this instance before you to show you what the true gold
of life is, that is, what gives *lasting worth* to any man's character
or labors. It is having *God* in them. Without God, they will both
perish; with God, they have a life long and blessed as God
himself. And David's short career shines today with a brighter
light than when it seemed to set in a little chamber in Northampton a century ago. "The poor young missionary is dead,"
they said. Ah no. He lives still, preaching on earth the blessed-
ness of God's redeeming love, and enjoying it to the full in
heaven. I hope you will get his whole history and read it.

GOOD FOR SOMETHING.

❦

"YOU are a good-for-nothing, that's what you are!" said a man in an angry tone to one of his sons. "Good for nothing! those chips are not picked up; that saw is on the ground for people to tumble over; the hens are in the garden, I dare say. Good for nothing! You don't earn your salt!"

"'Tisn't a very good world," muttered the boy.

"The world is good enough for the purpose for which it was built," answered his father, "and that is all anything is good for. A watch is good for time, a plough is good for turning up the soil, a ship is good for going to sea, a sheep for wool and mutton, a loom for one thing, an anvil for another; but it is hard telling what *you* are good for."

The boy was naturally neither expert nor handy, and his father's scolding did not make him any more so. Indeed it discouraged him. His mother too was dead, and the woman who took care of the house regarded him pretty much as his father did; James therefore received little or no encouragement from anyone, and he grew more and more careless and unhappy.

After this last talk, James determined to run away. "He wasn't any use to his father," he said; "and the sooner he was off the better." But could a good-for-nothing do better anywhere else than at home? No matter; go he would. So, instead of going to school the next day, he cut over the fields to a cross road leading to the next town. He got one ride that day, and the close of the day brought him to a farm-house, where he saw a man sharpening a large knife on the grindstone. James turned up to the shed. "Sha'n't I turn your grindstone for you, sir?" asked he. The man looked up with a friendly stare. "Well, yes," said he; "but who are you, pray?"

"A sort of good-for-nothing, that wants to be good for some-thing," answered the boy, whose day's reflections, I fancy, had begun to be profitable. Indeed he did think a great deal about the watch, and the plough, and the ship, and the sheep, and the loom, and the anvil being all good for something; while, poor he, what was he good for?

"That will do," said the man; "I don't see but you can turn a grindstone."

In a little further talk, James told him he was in quest of a place to live out, and the man asked him to stop a few days with him. "You say you are not good for much," said the man the next morning, "let's see you weed my onion bed;" so after breakfast the boy went to work. The sun grew pretty hot, and his back began to ache stooping over so, but he kept saying to himself, "I'll be a match for the weeds in this onion bed;" so he kept carefully on his work till the farmer came up from his field.

"Well, my boy, how do you get ahead?" James looked up, as much as to say, "How do *you* think, sir?" "Good for the onion bed," said the farmer; "tomorrow you may go down in the field and help me hoe potatoes." Tomorrow it rained, but the next day it cleared up, and James, with his hoe, followed the farmer. James at first made bungling work of it. He hoed down the young sprouts instead of hoeing up the earth. "That won't do," said the farmer. James saw plain enough that it would not, and tried to do better. He got tired after a few hills, and leaned on his hoe. The farmer looked up, but did not scold. He looked kind and said nothing. So James had leisure to think of the watch, and the plough, and the ship, and the sheep, and the loom, and the anvil, and presently took hold again, thinking he would at least try to be good for a potato hill. Upon the whole, the poor boy had a hard yet encouraging day of it. For it is true, in a large world like this where there is so much to do, everybody can find out, if they seriously try, that there is something they are good for. And James began that day to get a little glimpse that even he was good, or might be good, for something; and it was a considerable thing to find out.

After being at the farmer's a month, the man recommended him to his brother, who raised garden vegetables for the city market. "He's a boy that will come to something, sure," said the farmer to the gardener.

The farmer took pains to ride over and see James' father, but he was in a cross mood, for I suspect he had been drinking, and only gave the boy the character of being good for nothing "No harm in encouraging the lad," said the good-natured farmer.

"And no good," growled the father.

James went to live with the man, who raised garden vegetables for a green-grocer in the city. And after a while he was trusted to drive the morning cart in; it was an early cart, to have the vegetables in season for market. When he had driven it about a year, the green-grocer said to his head clerk, "I should like that James in our establishment; he is a boy good for something." "So should I," said the head clerk; "worth fifty common boys."

A proposition, in due time, was made to James, which the gardener, though sorry to lose him, advised him to accept; and we next find him a clerk in the city. The greengrocer was a pious man, and took James under his wing to church and Sabbath-school. James had not had much religious instruction. He always kept in his heart the little his poor sick mother taught him before she died, and he was pleased to find his Sabbath-school teacher talked like her. That made him eager to hear more. And when he found how the good Lord Jesus came into this world to save poor good-for-nothing sinners from their sins and the consequences of their sins in hell, his heart was melted, and he prayed the little prayer of the publican, "God be merciful to me a sinner."

James turned to Christ with a humble and believing heart, and a new joy filled his soul. Then he prayed the prayer of the young convert, "Lord, what wilt thou have me to do?" Oh, he longed to be good for something in the heavenly Master's service. Should the watch, the plough, the ship, the sheep, the loom, and the anvil serve the useful and important ends for which they were made, and he not pant to answer the nobler purpose for which God made him, which, as his catechism said, "is to glorify God and enjoy him for ever;" and to glorify God is to love him and to serve him with all our hearts, making his will and his law our chief delight.

James is now a devoted Christian merchant, good for everything his Master wants him for, ready with his time, his talents, and his money, to do good as he has opportunity.

WHAT RUINS THE BOYS.

"POOR boys have hard times of it." Do you not think their hard times are often their own making? I do. There was Alexander Downs, for instance, once a neighbor of mine, a smart boy, with a face to interest anybody. Alexander was a poor boy. His mother was a widow, and had to work hard for a living; but she was a good woman. Alexander had a pious mother. He had a good day-school, a good Sabbath-school, and a seat in church. There were friends ready to give him a new jacket, or cap, or pants, when his became ragged and his mother could not buy him clothes; and it is certain that a boy who is trying to do right will *never* be without people to befriend him. Alexander also had books from the Sabbath-school to read, and a neighbor always glad to lend him more. Yet for all this, Alexander played truant week-days, was seldom at his place in Sabbath-school, dodged his teachers, left the house of God, and in spite of the best advice and the kindest friends, step by step went down and down, herding with bad associates, until he broke open a store, and ended his short career in the state's prison.

And there are a dozen others whom I know going the same way, and thousands all over the land. They may not go to prison, but they will certainly be next door to it. What is the reason? Not ignorance. They know better, and I believe there are few boys that go down through ignorance. The reason is simple. They are "possessed"—possessed of a spirit, which, if it gets rule in a boy, is driving him on to certain ruin. What is it? The *spirit of disobedience*. The object of rules and restraints and laws, and teachers and masters and schools, is to keep down the bad in a boy's heart, by quickening and improving what is good. The spirit of disobedience reverses the order. It strives to *put out* the good by *letting loose* the bad; and it does it pretty thoroughly.

I have often thought how wonderful it is that we should have that single bit of the history of the Son of God when he was twelve years old—for twelve years is a very critical age in a boy's life. It is about the age when they begin to show their mettle, or rather, when we begin distinctly to hear the ring of it; and as Jesus shows us the true pattern of a boy, let us see what the leading spirit of it was, to teach all boys what it should be.

On a journey from the city of Jerusalem to their home in Galilee, his parents missed him. They hunted round among the crowd of travelers, and could not find him. Was Jesus lost? They turned and went back to the city, and at last found him in the temple, sitting with the learned men of the nation, both hearing them and asking them questions. And all that heard him were astonished at his understanding and his answers. When his mother told him they had sought him sorrowing, he asked if she did not know he "must be about his Father's business." It was not an idle curiosity, or a wish to break away from his parents, or a desire to take things into his own hands; but that sweet spirit of obedience to his Father in heaven, already showing itself in the boy, which shaped and directed his after years. "I seek not," he says, "mine own will, but the will of the Father which sent me." John 5:30. "My *meat*," he adds, "is to do the will of him that sent me, and to finish his work." John 4:34. "I do always those things that please him." John 8:29.

And because he knew he was set apart to do a great work for his Father in heaven, did he refuse to go back with his mother? Oh no. He went down with his parents to Nazareth, and *was subject* to them. Obedience to home restraints and parental authority was the marked thing in his boyhood.

"Suppose," says Dr. Todd, in one of his talks to children, "that a man now could dig up from under the ruins of the old temple at Jerusalem a true and exact picture of the boy Jesus as he sat in the midst of the doctors, hearing and asking them questions, and it could be *proved* that it was an exact portrait of him, how much money men would give for that picture! It would sell for a kingdom. And yet it would not be very valuable. It would be only a curiosity. The picture would not give us so good an idea of him as this beautiful story does. This shows him—his soul, his spirit—to us just as we want to see it. If we had had a picture of Christ, we might have worshipped it; or his disciples might think they were being like him if they wore their hair as he did, or dressed as he did, or wore their beard as he did. But now we know we are not like him unless we *feel* like him, *do* like him, and *think* like him. He has left us, not his picture, not the coat or the sandals that he wore, not a lock of hair, but something more precious. He left us his example, his beautiful example at twelve years old."

Gently his mother took him by the hand and led him towards their humble home. Meekly and quietly he walked by her side, perhaps now and then dropping a word about the great subjects he had been talking about with the doctors.

Will a boy love to go up to the house of God and listen to the teachings of his word, and hear about the great kingdom and glory of God? Yes, if he is like Jesus.

Will a boy who knows more about some things than even his mother, be ready to obey her, and love and honor her? Yes, if he is like Jesus.

Will a boy who can converse with great and learned men, and even astonish them, be willing to be subject to his mother, and be to her a kind and dutiful child? Yes, it he is like Jesus Christ our pattern, he will.

THE RIVER JORDAN.

WHAT river should you like best to visit? "The river Jordan," answers a little girl, "because my Savior was baptized there."

Every traveler to the Holy Land tries to visit it. It is about twenty-four miles from Jerusalem. As many robbers infest the caves and forests by the way, it is dangerous to undertake the journey from Jerusalem without a guard of soldiers. A curious custom takes place in the spring of every year, which it would be interesting to see—the bathing of the pilgrims in the Jordan.

Five, six, seven, or eight thousand people assemble at Jerusalem from many different lands to make a pilgrimage to this river. The Turkish governor escorts them with a guard of soldiers. They camp out on a large plain near Jericho. Two hours before daylight a rude kettle-drum rouses the sleeping multitude to begin their march to the river before the sun heats up the valley. Soon they are in motion. Before them are carried flaming torches, and all along huge watch-fires are kindled to light up the steep passes of the road. By the time the sun breaks over the hills the front rank reaches the river, which is a yellow, muddy stream, gliding between white cliffs and tamarisk and willow trees. In a short time the great body of the pilgrims come up on horses, asses, mules, and camels, some having whole families on their backs. On reaching the river they dismount, and set to work to take their bath in its waters, some on the open space, others further up among the thickets. Some plunge in naked; most, however, wear white dresses, which they bring with them. Though the number of men, women, and children is so large, good behavior everywhere prevails. In about two hours the shores are cleared; they quietly remount their beasts, and before the noon-day heat are again encamped on the upper plain of Jericho. At midnight the drum again beats for their homeward march. Torches again go before, and the people follow; and so quiet are they, that nothing but the clatter of hoofs and the tinkling of bells is heard. The troops stay on the ground till the last pilgrim is gone, and then the country becomes as desolate and silent as before.

What do they do it for? The poor pilgrims hope to wash away their sins in the Jordan, which they look upon as a holy river, forgetting, or not knowing that the blood of Christ alone cleanseth from all sin.

THE LIFE-CAR.

SEE that noble ship. She crossed the Atlantic with her precious cargo in safety. The merchants in New York were daily expecting her in port. The crew thought the worst of the voyage was over. Her passengers felt very near home, and talked briskly of seeing their fathers and mothers, their wives and children. "Tomorrow we shall go up the Narrows," said the captain.

But away in the far chambers of the east a storm is brewing. Dark clouds begin to fill the sky; the winds arise; the rain falls in torrents, and the waters are covered with angry waves. All night the storm increases; all night the ship is battered by the tempest. At last she strikes on the Jersey coast. A terrible sea staves in her bulwarks; her masts are shivered; her rudder is torn off; her life-boats are wrenched from their moorings. The brave old ship has battled many a tempest, but never one like this. The creaking and straining of her huge timbers are like the groans of a dying giant.

The morning light breaks on this awful scene, and the captain finds a terrible sea foaming and dashing between them and the land. The crew are doing their utmost; but it is little they can do now. Their noble ship, once so obedient to her helm, once so strong and beautiful, with her stately spars and snowy sails, is now a poor frail, unmanageable hulk. The passengers are pale with terror. Death stares them in the face. The ocean is ready to swallow them up. Must they perish—perish in sight of land— perish so near home? They strain their eyes to catch a sight of the green hills. They stretch out their hands, and cry, "Save us, O Lord, or we perish." The land, the land! What would they not give to reach it? The rich man would willingly become a beggar to set foot there. Oh, to stand in safety on that distant shore!

Their signals of distress have been heard. Their peril has been descried from the lighthouse. Men flocked to the beach. "To the rescue! to the rescue!" is the cry. But no boat can stem those angry waves. The stoutest swimmer cannot breast this fearful sea. Is there no other way of rescue? Moments are precious. The men on shore are hurrying to and fro. A cannon is brought to the beach, and a ball with a line fastened to it is fired over the ship. The line drops on the deck. The sailors catch and pull it in. It drags a hawser (a large cable) from the shore. A communication is now opened between ship and shore. What next? A life-car is hung from the hawser, by stout chains at its ends. A long pull, a strong pull, and a pull altogether from the men on the wreck. They work for their lives. The life-car reaches the ship. A shout of joy goes up from her decks.

What is a life-car? some may ask. It is a kind of boat made of copper or iron, and closed by a water-tight door, in which persons, three or four at a time, may be carried from a wrecked vessel to the shore. Do you think, when the life-car reached the sinking ship, that anyone said, "I am afraid to trust it; I doubt if it will hold. Perhaps it will drop me in the angry waves?" No, no; the passengers knew their danger too well. It was their only refuge. "I—I—I will go in the life-car;" and each was anxious to press into this way of escape. The women and children are put in first. The door is shut; it swings on the hawser, and rides over and above the raging sea; it nears the land; it reaches it in safety. Its precious freight is landed on the beach. Safe, safe! safe from the tempest; saved from a watery grave. This little life-car has been an ark of refuge, a hiding from the storm to many a tempest-tost crew and voyager on the dangerous shores of Jersey. In 1850, it safely landed two hundred passengers from a stranded ship, men, women, and little children.

What a wonderful invention is this life-car; so simple, and yet so great. What escape it offers; what a savior of lives has it been! Ah, yes; and as natural things so often remind us of eternal things, can we help pointing you to Jesus Christ, the life-car of the soul? Your soul is in as much greater danger than this ship's crew, as eternity is of more consequence than time. The waves of ungodliness are rising around you; the storm of God's displeasure against sin is beating upon you, and hell is ready to engulf you. There is a better land in sight. Can you reach it? Must you perish so near those blessed shores? You cannot cross those raging seas. Oh, no. But a life-car is provided. It comes to your rescue. Jesus Christ offers himself as an ark of refuge to every poor perishing sinner. Will you not trust yourself to him? Will you not commit yourself to the arms of his love, and be carried to the port of eternal safety? "Come unto me," he says, "and I will in no wise cast you out."

A STAGE-COACH INTERVIEW.

A FRENCH colporteur* not long ago took passage in a diligence—a French stage-coach—in which there were five other passengers. These men were briskly talking about religion, talking about it and scoffing at it in such a way as led the colporteur to think they knew very little about it. He, however, kept silent until one of them turned round and asked him what *he* had to say.

"Gentlemen," he said seriously, taking out his pocket Bible, "I am willing to believe that had you read this book, and given attention to the religion it teaches, you would have spoken of it with the respect it deserves."

"Oh, the Bible! the Bible!" they all cried, "that is a book of the priests."

"Gentlemen," replied the colporteur, "the Bible is the word of God, and you ought not to pass judgment upon it until you have read it. What you have not done I will now do." He then began to read from the gospels, and the time was taken up in reading and talk upon it until the diligence stopped. On parting with the colporteur, two of the travelers each bought a Bible; and one who had been loudest in scoffing, gave him his address, saying, "If possible, call upon me, and pray God to help me read and understand the one you have sold me, for I shall begin it at once."

A year after this, the colporteur passed through the village where this traveler lived, and made it a point to call at his farm, for the good man had not forgotten to pray often for him. As soon as he made himself known, the farmer fell on his neck and with the deepest feeling exclaimed, "Brother in Jesus Christ, welcome to my house, and rejoice with me. I have read that Bible, and have prayed. I have reread the Bible and prayed

*Colporteur—a seller or distributor of religious materials.

again, as you advised me, and as you said, light has arisen within me; the Bible has become to me the word of God—the word which, after showing me my wickedness, taught me what I must do to be saved. Brother, I believe Jesus Christ. Brother, rejoice with me. I have been made a child of God, though still feeble and very unworthy. I know in whom I believe." You may well suppose how the colporteur rejoiced, and what a delightful meeting it was.

As soon as this farmer had found religion, the religion of the Bible, he went to his old father and wanted to read the good book to him. "Are you then become a minister?" asked his father playfully. "No, I have become a Christian," answered the son; "and I shall have no rest, dear father, until you are one." Through the faithful efforts of his son, the old man also became a believer in Christ. Of this book so precious he bought thirty-five, and gave one to each of his family and intimate friends; and so the farmer labors on, himself a Bible society to all the district around, and what is better, his daily life is a living witness of its truth.

A CHILD'S FAITH.

"HOW sweet it is, my child,
  To live by simple faith;
Just to believe that God will do
  Exactly as he saith."

"Does faith mean to believe
  That God will surely do
Exactly what he says, mamma—
  Just as I know that you

Will give me what I ask,
  Because you love me well,
And listen patiently to hear
  Whatever I may tell?"

"Yes, you may trust in God,
  Just as you trust in me;
Believe, dear child, he loves you well,
  And will your Father be.

For when you sought his love,
  Your Father up in heaven
Looked kindly down for Jesus' sake,
  And has your sins forgiven.

To pray in faith, my child,
  Is humbly to believe
That what you ask in Jesus' name,
  You surely shall receive.

Go with your simple wants,
  And tell him all you need;
Go, put your trust in Christ alone;
  Such faith is sweet indeed."

THE SEA-SIDE.

THE children and their mother were going to the seaside to spend the forenoon: Jessie, who was the eldest, and Mary and little Fan and Bridget. Joseph, the farmer's son, who was going to the beach with his cart to get a load of kelp, said he would carry them part way; so they jumped in, and thought riding in a cart was about the pleasantest thing they ever did. Near the beach they got out, for Joseph was going another way after his kelp.

What is kelp? Sea-weed. After a storm great quantities of it are washed up on the coast, and the farmers cart it on their land for manure. It makes the land very rich.

The children and their mamma then walked through a belt of soft sand to the fine hard sand which forms the beach. "How smooth and pretty it is," cried Mary, running after the little waves, and running away from them, when they chased her back. "Oh! oh! oh!" cried the children, finding shells in plenty, for the storm had washed up a great many from the bottom of the sea, which was their home. Some were like gold; some like silver; some pink; some green, and some looked as if the rays of the setting sun had painted them so beautifully.

"Old ocean has emptied her lap full on this beach, I do believe," said Jessie.

"Oh no. Away down in the depth of the sea are millions of such, mingled with pearls and coral, and all as beautiful as possible," said their mamma.

"Why are they made so beautiful to live down there?" asked Jessie; "nobody ever sees or admires them. Fishes cannot admire them, and men never go there. Who can?"

"God can," answered her mother; "his mind planned every one; his hand formed every one; his skill painted every one; and

we are told, after God creates new things, 'he *rejoices* over all his work,' for they are the creations of his infinite wisdom."

"But they can't praise him," said Mary.

"Nor feel naughty," said little Fan, in a little low voice.

"Oh, how *finished* they are," cried Jessie, curiously examining a tiny shell. "This is only a baby shell in size, but it is as complete, and can bear the hard knocks of old ocean as well as the biggest shell you can find."

"It is different from *us* babies; isn't it, mamma?" said little Fan. "And, mamma, does God rejoice over *us* as well as over his shells? *we* are the works of his hand."

"Yes," answered the mother; "and more and more I hope he will have cause to. God rejoices over the little limbs, the bright eyes, the silky hair, the soft brow of the baby in its cradle. But when its little hands can do good, and its eyes melt in love and pity, and when its tongue can sing God's praises, and call upon him in prayer, God rejoices still more. And when the child becomes a woman, kind, excellent, faithful, loving her Savior and loving everybody else for her Savior's sake, a blessing to her family and everybody who knows her—and when she shall reach heaven at last, and leave all sin and sorrow behind, and go up in the white robes of Christ's righteousness, and come to her Redeemer with her song of praise, will not God *then* rejoice over his work? Other things, like shells, may show that God has given them graceful forms and beautiful colors; but the beauty of the Christian is the 'beauty of the Lord,' which is the beauty of holiness."

"I hope that will be *our* beauty," whispered Mary; "and if we find a pearl, I hope it will be the pearl of great price; for God rejoices over that, does he not, mamma?"

And so this pious mother and her children wandered up and down the beach, filling their baskets with shells, sitting on the rocks and watching the waves chasing each other up and down the smooth sand, all the while sweetly talking, and the mother ever quietly weaving, in her web of talk, thoughts of the blessed God.

THE GOOD VOYAGE.

A SAILOR'S STORY.

"I JOINED the United States service on board a man-of-war," said he, "and went to sea, not caring where the ship was bound. At sea we were caught in a gale of wind, when three days' sail from Rio. Our masts went by the board. We were on a lee-shore, and were expecting every moment to find a watery grave. Then I remembered the prayers of my father, and how, when I was a little child, he used to kneel with me at the bed-side and give me to God. This came up before me, and when the captain said, 'We shall soon be swept into eternity,' I felt I was lost for ever. I kneeled down on deck, and prayed to God to have mercy on me; and I made a vow that if he would spare my life, I would give myself to his service.

"We were saved; but I did not keep my vow. No, it was bro-ken. But his goodness followed me. I was taken sick, and again, in my lonely bunk, I thought of him. I prayed for his forgiveness through the Lord Jesus Christ. The ship went to the Sandwich Islands. There a missionary came on board. I was sitting on deck. He came up and asked me, 'Do you read your Bible?' 'I have none, sir,' I said; 'I suppose there is one in the ship, but I do not read it.' He then gave me a New Testament, and said, 'I pray God that it may be blest to your soul.' I read that Testa-ment after the godly man left. I read it a great deal, but did not find the comfort I expected. At length I came to the passage, 'God so loved the world that he gave his only begotten Son, that whosoever believeth in him should not perish, but have ever-lasting life.'

"There was no closet where I could go, so I knelt down on the deck of the vessel, and there, blessed be God, he spoke peace to my soul. I went and told my shipmates, thinking they would be glad. But they thought I was crazy. They teased and laughed at me. I tried to do good to my shipmates. The first thing I did was to pray God for them. Then I could talk. One night I was lean-ing on the anchor-stock, thinking of the goodness of my God. I repeated the hymn,

"'Alone, yet not alone am I.'

It was a beautiful moonlight night, and I said to my God, 'I have no one to sing with me, no one to pray with me. Give me a kid to make merry.' He heard my prayer. Two days after, a sailor on board came to me, and said, 'John, I am miserable.' 'What is the matter, Joe?' I asked. 'Ah, John,' he said, 'some-thing is the matter here,' putting his hand to his heart. 'I was brought up in a Sunday-school. I know you are right, John.' I said to him, 'The blood of Jesus can save you.' We began to read and pray together, and soon he was made happy in the Lord.

"Soon after this, while we were sitting in the bow of the ship, we sang the 'Star of Bethlehem,' and asked God for another to keep us company. And he gave us another. Then did our hearts rejoice. Soon four or five more were brought to God through faith in his Son. Many were angry at the good work. One sailor could give up everything but *rum.* He could not part with that. He said he should like to be a Christian, and wanted to know how he might be one. I said to him, 'If you want to be a Chris-tian, you must give up your sins.' 'I will give up my sins,' he said. 'Will you give up rum?' 'No,' he replied, 'I cannot give up rum. I *will* drink my two glasses of rum. Can't a man be a Christian,' said he, 'without giving up rum?' I told him perhaps it might be, but that God had said, 'Woe unto him who riseth early in the morning to drink strong drink.' I told him I would not drink a drop, if the commodore himself should offer me a glass. Well, that man wouldn't give up his rum, and so when he went ashore two glasses led to more. He was taken to a trap of hell in Water-street, and he is now lying in the churchyard, without a stone to mark the spot, far away from home and friends. Ah, God follows men on the sea more closely than the winds follow the ship."

This story of a converted sailor on one of the United States ships during a recent cruise, is interesting on many accounts. Does it not say, "Sow the seed?" Sow the good seed in the hearts of the young; never be discouraged; never despair. It will spring up at times and seasons you little think of, and may never know. The prayers of pious parents, the instructions of faithful Sabbath-school teachers, are not lost.

UNDER THE FIG-TREE.

I F you found a wedge of gold, how you would run to show it to
your father and mother, your brothers and sisters. If you make
a new acquaintance, how anxious you are to introduce your
friends to him, and have them enjoy his society also. It is natural
for us to wish our friends to share our enjoyment with us.

I suppose Philip felt so, when he found that Jesus Christ was
the very Savior which the Bible promised to men. He was glad;
and he went directly and told his friend Nathanael, "We have
found Him of whom Moses and the prophets did write, Jesus of
Nazareth, the son of Joseph."

"Can any good thing come out of Nazareth?" asked Nathanael, for it was a wicked city. Philip did not stop to argue about
it. "Come and see" for yourself, he said, knowing how much
better satisfied people are to judge for themselves than by
hearsay. Nathanael went with Philip. When Jesus saw him
coming, he said, "There is a sincere and upright man." How did
Jesus know? "How do you know me?" asked Nathanael. "Before
Philip called you, when you were under the fig-tree, I saw you,"
answered the Lord Jesus.

Nathanael instantly felt that he was no stranger to Jesus of
Nazareth. Something took place under the fig-tree which showed
his true character. He thought he was alone. He thought no eye
saw him. Perhaps he went out under its quiet and cooling shade
to pray. The Jews often chose such places for secret prayer. But
the eye of Jesus of Nazareth pierced into his privacy, and it read
his secret thoughts and feelings. Nathaniel's conscience told him
that he was in the presence of an all-seeing Being; and this was
proof enough that he could not be a mere man: he was indeed the
long-expected Savior. "Master," cried the young man, convinced,
"thou art the Son of God; thou art the King of Israel."

Jesus, children, sees us when we least expect it. Do you try to hide anything from your mother? You cannot hide it from the Lord Jesus. Do you mean to deceive your father? You cannot deceive the Lord Jesus. If you mutter a wicked word, he hears it; if you harbor a bad thought, he knows it. He searches your heart, and follows you all the day through. You are never alone; you are never out of his sight. The wicked try to flea from his presence; but they never, never can. This is a great comfort, if you live in such a way as not to be afraid of Jesus' eye. This is a comfort which all his friends have. If they are wrongfully blamed, or ill-treated, or neglected, or oppressed, they are sure that Jesus knows it all. He will judge right. He will protect and defend them, and bring out everything right at last. He counts all your tears, and hears all your sighs.

"It's dark, and we've not a drop of candle, and daddy can't see me, and mother can't see me, but Jesus Christ can; he'll watch me," said a poor sick boy one dark, cold night, taking comfort in the watchful eye above.

How is it with you? Jesus of Nazareth is in heaven now; but he sees you, just as he saw Nathanael under the fig-tree. What does he find you doing? Nathanael was not afraid to have Christ look at him. Are you, my little one?

THE HEART'S BURDEN.

ONE Sabbath morning I read to Emma the first part of Pilgrim's Progress. She listened with deep attention. The burden on Christian's back greatly interested her, and as if a feeling of a similar experience of her own were gradually quick-ening into life, she sighed, "Poor, poor Christian, how heavy it must have been."

By and by she came to me, when I had laid aside the book and had gone to my room; with a look which I cannot describe, her whole soul seeming to look out of her eyes, she asked, "Mamma, *is* there any burden on my back? Is there any on yours, and on papa's?" I replied by asking, "Did you ever *feel* one?" "Oh, mamma, I do not know; but *is* there?" "Yes, we have each one burden," I replied, "the little child no less than the father and the mother. You know, dear, what that burden is, do you not?" She looked up wistfully. "Is it sin?" she asked.

Yes, it is sin. Little children, do you never *feel* its burden on your heart? Do you never know a pain and anxiety which you cannot explain? When the task is done and the lesson said, and there is nothing more but play, does it not sometimes come back, this dull, aching sense of something wrong? When the Sabbath evening stillness comes, when you lie thinking in the night, do you not feel it? It is the *burden of sin*. It is the heavy burden which every child heart and every older heart must bear until Jesus takes it away. You know that no one could take it from Christian's back till he had come to the cross, and then it rolled away. There is no other way for us but Christian's way. Go to Jesus, to the cross he died on, and there our faith will see it roll away and hide for ever in his grave.

Does any little child know what it is to have this burden

lifted from the heart? Nathan Dickerman knew; little Henry in India knew; and many children who live to grow up, know also how light and joyful that heart is whose burden Jesus has taken away. Little child, do not carry this heavy burden any longer; Jesus is waiting to take it from you.

THE HEAVENLY VOICE.

AFTER Jesus Christ was twelve years old, the Scriptures give us but little about his history until he was thirty. What was he doing all that time? We know what he was *not* doing. Through all his youth he never did a single thing to be sorry for. He never said a word or did an act unworthy or unbecoming the highest excellence of character. Oh, let every young person study such an example.

Before Christ entered on his public ministry, God sent a man to the Jews to tell them that his Son was soon coming to be their Savior. This man was John the Baptist. And he said to all the people, "Repent, for the kingdom of heaven is at hand." Jesus left Nazareth, where he had lived with his parents, and went to John, who was preaching and baptizing in the river Jordan, that he might be baptized by John. Did John know who Jesus was? He thought he was the Son of God. But the people did not know him. Do you know who told them? God himself. Jesus when he was baptized went up out of the water, and the sky opened over his head, and the Spirit of God descended like a dove and lighted on him, and a voice from heaven was heard, saying, "This is my beloved Son, in whom I am well pleased." It was the heavenly Father's voice.

"Don't you think it was a very *kind* voice?" asked a little boy at my side; "I wish I could hear the heavenly Father's voice." Oh, yes, it is very kind to all who love his dear Son Jesus Christ. He sent him down to this wicked world to save people from their sins, and make them holy and happy, and bring them home with him to heaven. Will you not love the Son of God and obey him, and be one of his dear followers? Then God will make you his child, and his voice will sweetly whisper in your heart, "This also is my beloved son for Jesus' sake."

THE OLD HERB WOMAN.

ALICE found her one day resting under the cooling shade of a tree outside the garden-gate.

"Do you want something?" asked Alice.

"Yes, dear child," she answered, "I want a new dress."

"A pretty calico?" asked Alice. "That will too soon fade," answered the poor herb woman. "A black woolen?" asked Alice. "That will too soon wear out," answered she. "A silk?" asked Alice. "I have nothing fit to wear with it," answered the herb woman, and Alice thought as much. "A plaid, a beautiful plaid?" asked the child. "That will too soon go out of fashion," answered the herb woman. "Do you care much about the fashion?" asked Alice. "I want the dress to last me a thousand years or more," said the old woman.

"Oh," exclaimed Alice, drawing back, for she half thought the poor woman was crazy, "do you expect to live so long? A thousand years is a great, great while, and you are pretty old now."

"I shall live longer than that," said she.

"I will ask my mother," said the little girl, much puzzled, "if she knows what dress would suit you, and perhaps she'll buy it for you."

"Your mother is not rich enough to buy it, dear child," said the old woman.

"My *father* is rich," said she.

"Not rich enough to buy me the dress I want," answered the old woman.

"Do you want to dress like a queen?" asked Alice.

"No; but I want to be dressed like a King's daughter."

"The old herb woman *is* crazy," thought Alice to herself; "she talks so queer." "I don't know where you will get such a dress," said she aloud, "something that will never fade, never wear out, never go out of fashion."

"And never get soiled or spoiled," added the old herb woman; "wear it when and where you may, it will always keep white and shining."

"Oh," was all Alice could say. Then she added, "*I* should like such a one, I am sure. Could a little girl have one? But a little girl would outgrow hers."

"No," said the herb woman, "the dress would let itself out so as to suit you always."

The child was lost in wonder. "Will you please tell me what it is, and where I can get one?" she asked.

It is the garment of salvation, the robe of righteousness, which Jesus Christ has wrought out for you and for me, dear child," said the old woman tenderly. "Christ came to take away the poor rags of our sins, and to put on us his pure white robes, and make us fit to be children of God, the great King, and live in his palace for ever. Should you not like to, dear child?"

"Yes," answered the child, "I do want to be one of God's children. I always wanted to. Will he give *me* a heavenly dress, do you think?"

THE CROCODILE AND ICHNEUMON.

A CROCODILE of great size and fierceness infested the banks of the Nile, and spread terror and desolation through all the country round. He ate up the shepherds and the sheep, the herdsmen and the cattle together. Everybody fled from before him. Various plans were devised and many efforts made for his destruction, but in vain. A public meeting of the inhabitants was held, to consider what should be done to rid the country of this plague. While they were consulting together, the ichneumon stepped forth, and thus addressed them. The ichneumon is a small animal, and lives on crocodile's eggs.

"I see your distress," said the ichneumon; "and though I cannot assist you in your present difficulty, yet I can offer you some advice that may be of use to you for the future. A little prudence is worth all your courage; it may be glorious to overcome a great evil, but the wisest way is to prevent it. You despise the crocodile while he is small and weak; but when he gains his full size and strength, you fear him and flee from him. You see I am a poor little feeble creature, yet I am much more terrible to the crocodile and more useful to the country than you are. *I attack him in the egg:* while you are contriving, for months together, how to get rid of one crocodile, and all to no purpose, I effectually destroy fifty of them in a day."

> This fable, dear child, is intended to show
> The danger of suffering ill habits to grow;
> For the fault of a week may be conquered, 'tis clear,
> Much easier than if it went on for a year.

Yes, children, take a lesson from the wise little ichneumon. When you find out a bad habit or evil temper, *attack it in the egg.* Don't wait till, like the crocodile, it grows so strong and fierce that you can do nothing with it. And do not do this in your own strength. Pray for Jesus to help you. Without him we can do nothing.

ROCK.

"SOLID as a rock." "Firm as a rock." Solidity and firmness are the two chief virtues of rock. You stand upon rock, and it does not slide away like sand, or crumble like clay, or sink like marsh or quagmire. It is *sure*. Therefore rock is used as a foundation to build upon. There is a lighthouse at the mouth of our harbor, half a mile from the shore, of which, the moment you saw it, you would think as Willie said, "Why, it grows on the water." No, it is built on a rock, a sunken ledge, where many a poor ship had been wrecked before it was built. In violent storms the winds shake it and the waves dash furiously against it, but it stands, for it is founded on a rock. And the two solitary men who keep the light burning through the long, dark winter nights, feel as secure as you in your bed, for they know it is founded on a rock.

The Bible, using a great variety of ways to describe God, calls him a rock. "Who is a rock, save our God?" cries David; "the rock of my salvation," my rock of refuge. Why is he called so? Because he is so *sure*. He can always be depended upon. What God threatens will surely come to pass. What he promises he will certainly make good. If you trust him he will never fail you. Father, mother, friends, business, riches, health may fail you, but God never. He is a rock, firm and solid as the everlasting hills.

But God in Christ our Savior is a special rock;
A ROCK CLEFT:

> "Rock of ages, cleft for me."

Dying on the cross, that I might live. Cleft, and yet made a "corner-stone," as St. Paul tells us. As the corner-stone is the chief stone in a foundation, so Jesus Christ is the corner-stone in Christianity. All true piety must rest on the forgiveness of sins through his blood, which takes away sin. Are you building your character and all your daily life on that, dear child? Are you truly praying that little prayer, "Oh God, forgive my sins for Christ's sake?" If so, you have laid a sure foundation: build on it love, joy, peace, long-suffering, gentleness, goodness, faith, meekness, temperance. This is your life-house, not made with hands. The rains may descend and the floods come, and the winds blow and beat upon that house, but it will not fall, for it is founded upon a rock.

SAFE HIDING-PLACE.

A FAT mother hen was one day strutting on the green, with her chickens running merrily about her pecking and peeping, as happy as any happy family could well be. Suddenly she caught sight of a dark spot in the sky. What a cry of terror came from her little throat. How the frightened chicks rushed in an instant under her wings. How bristling and fierce the old hen looked. What was the matter? Ah, it was a hawk in the air, out getting his breakfast, and ready to dive at some unwary chicken. But every chick is safe and snug under its mother's wings. The hungry hawk was loath to go. "I will die before you shall seize one of my little ones," the old hen seemed to say in every feather of her body and every look of her eye. The hawk soon saw it was no use, and in a few moments flew away. She then gave a note of joy and triumph, and out hopped the chickens from their secure hiding-place; some hesitating, as if not quite over their fright; others, more bold, stepping confidently off. Ah,

they knew those warm and friendly wings were ready at a moment's notice to shelter them again.

Do you remember what the Lord Jesus once said to Jerusalem in the twenty-third chapter of Matthew? He loved Jerusalem. He knew that enemies wanted to destroy it. He desired to save it. But no; the people would not mind his warning cries, and one morning as he stood looking at the city, he said, "Oh, Jerusalem, Jerusalem, how often would I have gathered thee, *as a hen gathereth her chickens under her wings.* "

The blessed Savior, you see, is a refuge from harm. He is a sure refuge, an instant refuge, a warm refuge, a loving refuge. He cares for the "little ones," for he says, "Suffer little children to come unto me." Under the refuge of Jesus, we shall be safe from the attacks of sin and of Satan, that like hungry birds of prey, are always ready to pounce upon us.

A PERSECUTED FLOCK

֍

THE men have left their workshops and farms, the women their kitchens and dairies, and the little children their play, to come to this by and lonely spot to hear about Jesus Christ, their Savior and Friend. Why did they come hither? Have they no church?

These people are a company of French peasants. They live in a group of five small hamlets, called Ville-Favard. Once they had no preaching, and no schools; they were ignorant of Bible truth, and therefore very superstitious. When their cattle were sick, they hung little bags of consecrated salt around their necks to cure them. When sick themselves, they went or sent to some favorite saint to heal them of their diseases. The only person who could read or write was a peasant in wooden shoes and a cotton cap, who, for some small pay, wrote and read their letters; but I suppose their correspondence was little enough.

By and by a colporteur with his pack of Bibles on his back strayed into this district. He went from cottage to cottage and asked the people if they did not want a Bible. A Bible; what was that? A Bible was a good book, the best of books, the book of books, but alas, they could not read. What were they to do? Then the colporteur read to them from the Bible. I suppose he read, "Come unto me, all ye that labor and are heavy-laden, and I will give you rest." And he told them that He who made the promise, could make *good* his promise; for it was the Son of God, the precious Savior who shed his blood to wash their sins away; and all they had to do was to *come* to him. What good words; what sweet words! And they wanted more read, and more, and then they wished to learn to read for themselves. "Oh, this is just the Savior we want," they said. The colporteur

supplied them with Bibles, promising to speak in their behalf to the Evangelical Society in Paris to send them teachers. He did so, and teachers came down to Ville-Favard; and they opened day-schools and Sabbath-schools, and preached the blessed gospel. Oh, it was a good time in the little hamlets. Many, many now found just what they always longed for—a Savior, to save them from their sins, a heavenly Helper and Comforter. They were so happy. And other villages heard the glad tidings, and shared the blessing.

At last the opposers of the Bible found out how things were going on, and they were very angry. "Down with Bible schools, and away with Bible preaching," they cried. A great persecution began. They got the officers and magistrates on their side, and shut up the schools, closed their chapel doors, and forbade the reading of the Bible. "*We* will provide schools and churches; you may go to *ours*," said these enemies of the word of God.

What did the poor villagers do? Give up their precious Bible truth? This they could never do; the police officers might indeed break up their meetings, but they could not root the gospel out of their hearts; no, they could not do that. And they used to gather together secretly in the woods and by-places. This picture was taken by one of their teachers. And do you see that man on the hill yonder? He is stationed to keep a look-out for the police agents, who scour the country on horseback with a pack of dogs to break up their meetings, and arrest the preachers and teachers.

One of these little congregations continued to keep together for three years, dodging their enemies by moving from place to place, but was at last discovered by the bloodhounds, and condemned to pay a fine of two thousand francs, or about four hundred dollars—an immense sum for these poor people.

They are still in trouble. But Christ keeps watch over his little flock, and he says to them as to all his crushed and persecuted people everywhere, "Fear not, little flock; for it is your Father's good pleasure to give you the kingdom." Greater is He that is with them, than they who are against them.

THE BLIND BOY'S PATIENCE.

T HE other day I went to see a little blind boy. The scarlet-fever settled in his eyes, and for many months he has not seen at all. He used to be a sprightly little fellow, upon the run everywhere. "Well, my dear boy," I said, "this is hard for you, is it not?" He did not answer for a minute, then he said, "I don't know as I ought to say *hard;* God knows best;" but his lip quivered, and a little tear stole down his cheek.

"Yes, my child, you have a kind heavenly Father, who loves you and feels for you more even than your mother does." "I know it, sir," said the little boy, "and it comforts me." "I wish Jesus was here to cure Frank," said his little sister; "Jesus cured a good many blind men when he was on earth, and I am most sure he would cure Frank." "Well," said I, "he will open little Frank's eyes to see what a good Savior he is. He will show him that a blinded heart is worse than a blind eye, and he will wash his heart in his own blood, and cure it, and make him see and enjoy beautiful heavenly things, so that he may sit here and be a thousand times happier than many children who are running about."

"I can't help wishing he could see," said Lizzie. "I dare say," said I, "but I hope you don't try to make Frank discontented."

"Frank *isn't* discontented," said Lizzie earnestly; "he loves God."
"And love sets everything right, and makes its own sunshine;
does it not, Frank?" "I don't feel cross now," said the little blind
boy meekly; "when I'm alone, I pray, and sing my Sabbath-
school hymns, and sing, and sing, and God's in the room; and it
feels light, and—and—I forget I'm blind at all;" and a sweet
light stole over his pale features as he spoke; it was heavenly
light I was sure. I went to pity and comfort him, but I found
God had gone before me. The great God who has a thousand
worlds to take care of, did not overlook him, but with his heart
of love came and turned his mourning into joy, his darkness
into light, and made him in his misfortunes as happy as a child
can be. Oh, God can do more and better for us than we can ask
or think.

THE DRINKING FOUNTAIN.

"T HE Drinking Fountain movement is making great progress," says an English paper. Good. What is it? you may
ask; for though you have probably heard about it, you may have
forgotten. It is the plan of erecting fountains in the hot and
dusty cities and thoroughfares, where men, women, and children, dogs, horses, and cattle can have a cool draught of pure
water to slake their thirst. A drink of water is one of the greatest of blessings. Many a poor horse has died for the want of it;
many a poor dog has run mad for the want of it; many a poor
laborer has gone to the ale-house and gin-shops, because it was
easier to get these than a drink of water. A thoughtful regard
for these has lately run into a fountain; sometimes erected by
one benevolent gentleman or lady; sometimes by the city au-
thorities, like this in Salford; sometimes by the workmen themselves, as when it was proposed by some kind people to set a
subscription on foot for one to be put in the market-square at
Oldham. "No," said the working-men, "these fountains are for
our benefit; let us have the privilege of building it from our own
earnings;" and they accordingly did. Here is a picture of it.

Last summer we were detained at a railroad station, and
wore away the time by looking about. One object of interest was
a cattle-pen, for this was a point where cattle were sent to the
great cattle markets. It was half full of cattle. The day was hot
and sultry, and the poor creatures were panting with heat and
thirst, and there was no well or trough, or any appliances for
giving them drink. We presume this want is supplied at some of
the stations, but here they were suffering. At the Chichester
station, the drinking-troughs for cattle "are made great use of
on market-days by hundreds of live stock," says the dépôt-
master, "and they are of *very great use*." They are cheaply built,

and fed by a tank-pipe from the tank which supplies water to the locomotives. God has so abundantly supplied us with water, and it is so vital to our comfort, that we ought not to stint it to man or beast.

If you ever travelled in Vermont in the old chaise times, you remember the troughs found by the roadsides fed by the mountain rills, where your poor horse thankfully stopped and took a cool drink to refresh him for a quick trot over the next hill. They bespoke such a friendly people nestling among the hollows.

These fountains are good, very good—pure, free, life-giving, ever-flowing; so that no wonder the prophet Zechariah likened the *best* thing we can ever have to a fountain. The salvation brought us by Christ is called, as you know, a *"fountain* opened for sin and all uncleanness." That is the best fountain. Oh, may we bathe in it and be cleansed; may we drink of it and be saved.

THE CORN AND THE THISTLE.

HERE is a kernel of corn. How hard and dry and old it is! Is it good for anything? Oh yes, it is good to plant; it looks old and withered, but it is alive: put it in the ground, and see if it will not sprout; there is enough in that hard yellow kernel to make you rich.

To make me rich!

Yes; plant it, it will come up and bear four ears perhaps; each ear may yield two hundred kernels: plant all these kernels again, and you may have one hundred and thirty hills of corn; what was only one hill the first year will be one hundred and thirty hills the second year, and so on until in a few more years you will have a plenty of corn to eat, enough for your pigs and hens, besides a great deal for the market—so much is wrapped up in the inside of this kernel. A whole field of corn! Why, it is a precious, good little kernel; it is worth a great deal.

Now go and fetch me a thistle-seed. "Oh, I am afraid to go near the thistle; it will prick my hands and feet; it stings like a wasp." Try and get one. Here, I have got one, two, three; I picked them off and run. The thistle-seed is light and airy; it is long and slender, with fine down at one end, like wings; the winds waft it along; it looks prettily floating about in sunshiny weather. But nobody welcomes the thistle-down; nobody wishes to see it alight in their garden; no, no.

Let us go into the garden. The gardener has been very busy; he has been digging, hoeing, raking the earth, until it is now fit to plant. The sun shines warm on the beds. Let us find a warm spot for our corn. Here is one: our hills shall be in company with other hills. Get the hoe—that will do; now drop in the kernel. Cover it up. We will leave it in the dark, moist earth. Poor little kernel. When it comes up, will it sprout up a thistle, I wonder?

"A thistle!" cries the little boy, "a thistle? no, indeed; corn come up a thistle? it will come up just what it is planted: if it is planted a good, sweet kernel, it will be good, sweet corn by and by." Well, let us leave it.

Where shall we plant the thistle? "Oh, do not plant that; our garden is too nice for a thistle; it will sting all the little flowers near it; it yields no fruit; it will do no good at all, it will do harm, for it takes the place of something better." Stop; perhaps it will come up corn. "How strange you talk! a thistle-seed come up corn? a thistle-seed must come up a thistle; it will come up just what it is planted, good or bad. Corn comes up corn; thistles come up thistles." Are you sure? Find a corner to plant it in, and we will see what it comes up. Open the ground and drop it in.

Cover it up lightly. We will now leave it to the rain and the sun and the juices of kind mother earth.

Ralph grew quite impatient. One day he thought he would peep into the cornhill, to see how the little kernel fared. He opened the ground carefully with his fingers; soon he espied it. It looked quite dark and dead. For a minute Ralph was disappointed; but as he looked a little more closely, he saw something bursting out. It was the sprout, full of life, just ready to find its way to the light and air above its head. Ralph was pleased; he covered it quickly up, and waited until it peeped through the ground. One rosy morning beheld its green tips; the next day it was a tiny blade: it looked pale and timid, but the sun smiled upon it and it took courage. After that, it grew and grew as fast as could be. "You see the corn has come up corn." Yes, it has. The thistle too did well. "The thistle came up a thistle." Yes, so it did. It was warm, summer weather, and everything in the garden thrived.

In company with its neighbors, our corn became a tall and noble stalk. Its long leaves waved gracefully in the wind: its little ears began to show themselves, wrapped up in their warm silk blanket. Every day they became rounder and fuller. Soon it was fit for food. A large plate of corn appeared upon the table; some of our ears were among the rest; everybody had a bite; the kernels were full and juicy; they were sweet and rich to the taste. "The corn is very good," they said; "we must increase the stock—it is fine corn indeed." Neighbor Thompson saw some. "It is excellent," he cried. "You must let me have some kernels for next year; it is worth a great deal." The pigs grunted over the cobs, as much as to say, "Sweet cobs! juicy cobs! good cobs! more cobs!" The stalks and the leaves were carefully gathered and cast to the cows; the cows chewed them; never a better cud had they. Not any part of the corn was lost or wasted, or cast away good for nothing. In a cold autumn afternoon the children parched some; the little kernels bounded out of the pan, white and crisp and very tempting. "Oh, what beautiful parched corn!" they all cried at once. "We must fill our garden with it next year," said the gardener, as he carefully put by the ripest ear.

But the thistle, where was that? It grew rank and prickly: it crowded all its useful and excellent neighbors; biting them whenever it could. The gardener said he would never let such a vile thing grow in his garden again. He cut it down, and threw it over the fence to die. The pigs and the cows ran away from it.

But why did not the thistle come up corn? "It could not," cries Ralph, "never was such a thing heard of, never; things come up just what they are planted. A thistle must come up a thistle."

Is this really so, Ralph? Do things come up just what they are planted? Is it only the good seed which brings forth the good fruit, and does the bad seed bring forth only bad fruit? This is a great truth. The Bible says, "Whatsoever a man soweth, that shall he also reap." The Bible applies it to ourselves, as well as to plants. Then it becomes a very solemn truth. Do you know that, by and by, *you* will be put into the grave, and your body will be covered up by the cold earth? But your body will not lie there for ever; there is wrapped up within something that never dies: it is the soul, which must burst its narrow limits; and it will live for ever; the soul is life, and it cannot die.

As things in the natural world *come up just what they are planted*—corn comes up corn, and thistle comes up thistle—so it is in the moral world: if you go down to the grave bad boys, bad girls, you will live again bad boys, bad girls; the grave makes no

change in the character of your souls. If you go down to the grave good boys, good girls, with your sins forgiven and your souls washed in the Savior's blood, you will arise and live again holy children.

Here the good and bad grow together, like the corn and the thistle. But when they arise and live again, they will be parted for ever. Holy children, whose souls have been made pure in the blood of the Lamb, will dwell and flourish in that beautiful garden of the Lord, which is heaven. And the bad, they will be plucked up and cast away with the devil and his angels.

It is a solemn thought. *As you die, so will you live again.* In the grave the sinful cannot become holy, nor will the holy become sinful. There can be no change in the grave. How do you mean to die, children? you shudder at the thought of going to the grave a sinful child: "Let me die the death of the good," you say. This day then, *today* become a penitent, God-fearing, obedient, holy child. Death and the grave may come soon; then it will be too late. A thistle must be a thistle, and the corn, corn—for ever.

LOOK.

"LOOK!" Not run, but look; not go, but look; not stop, but look—look! A great deal depends upon looking.

A boy once had a fine knife, an English knife, with a Sheffield blade, a present from his uncle. He went into the woods one day, and lost it. Not till he reached home was it missed. The poor little fellow felt bad enough. Besides the loss, he was ashamed of his carelessness. What could he have been thinking of? "Go back and look," said his father. "It's of no use, I know," said the boy. "Look, look!" repeated his father. He went, and after a careful search the knife was found under a sassafras bush. *Looking* found the knife.

A packet-ship crossing the Atlantic was nearing the coast. For some days the weather had been lowering. Neither sun nor stars were visible, and no observation had been taken. There was a heavy swell. The log was carefully noted, but the exact whereabouts of the ship could not be ascertained. The mate took soundings, and a sailor was aloft on the look-out. "Breakers ahead!" shouted the man from the mast-head. "Ready about!" thundered the man at the helm. The ropes rattled, the sails flapped heavily, while the bow swung round to the larboard, and the noble ship plunged off from her perilous course. Night set in. Anxious eyes were strained towards the dark and gloomy horizon. The captain consulted his chart. There was a light he ought to make. Where was he drifting to lose it? "Light!" shouted the look-out from the masthead. A distant glimmer was discovered. The ship's bearing was ascertained. Alarm and anxiety gave way to hope and joy. *Looking* saved the ship.

The Bible says, "Look!" Look; where? Look; to whom? Look; why? "Look unto Me, and be ye saved." Who says this? Who is

ME? Moses? No; for he says, "I can no more go out or come in." David? No; for he says, "My flesh and my heart faileth." Who? Solomon, the great king? No. "Look not unto me," he says; "put not your trust in princes." Who? John? No; for he says, "He that cometh after me is preferred before me." Who? Paul? No; for he says, "I am less than the least of all saints." Who then?

Moses declares, "The Lord is my strength and my song, and he is become my salvation." David answers, "In the Lord do I put my trust. He is the strength of my heart, and my portion for ever." John says, "Behold the Lamb of God, which taketh away the sin of the world." Paul adds, "I can do all things through Christ strengthening me. I count all things but loss for the excellency of the knowledge of Jesus Christ my Lord." "Me!" Who? It is the Lord, our Christ and Savior. "Look unto me," he says, "and be saved."

And everybody who has looked says he can make good his promise. He can save from sin, for his "blood cleanseth from all sin." He can save from hell, for he whispers to every dying penitent, "Today thou shalt be with me in paradise." He can save us from feeling troubled, for he says, "My peace I give unto thee." He can save us from worrying and giving up, for he says, "My grace is sufficient for thee." He can save us from being lonely when our dearest friends go away or die, for he says, "I will never leave thee, nor forsake thee."

What a Savior we have to look to! You have found, dear children, if you think at all, how many things you have looked to have failed and disappointed you already. Everything in this world will, sooner or later; but Jesus never, never will. Oh how sweet to have such a friend to look to, and to look to him for everything. Our dear parents and friends can only distribute what *he* gives.

Take home then to your hearts today this one little word, "Look." "Look unto *me*, and be ye saved." Isa. 45:22.

THE NEW SHIELD.

"THIS is New Year's Day at last, mother, and I am so happy. Such beautiful presents! How can I thank you and father enough? See all these beautiful books, and then this box of tools. I never can be idle a moment;" so said little Henry Grey as he stood surveying his new treasures very earnestly. "And oh, mother," he continued, "I am so glad it is New Year's Day, for I want to *begin right;* I want to be a good boy all the time, everywhere—much better than I was last year."

"I am very glad that you want to begin right, Harry," said his gentle mother as she kissed the rosy cheeks of her little son. "No New Year's gift could make me so happy as your earnest endeavor to become a good boy."

"Well, mother, when I looked at all these beautiful things, I said to myself, I ought to be a better boy, when I have such a kind father and mother, and so many friends."

"Who gave you your father and mother and friends, Harry? Whom ought you to serve and thank first of all for these blessings?"

"God," answered Harry in a low voice; "but, mother, I do so many things that are not right. Sometimes you and father do not find them out; but does God always know, mother? It makes me afraid when I think about that."

"God does indeed know all we do and say. He is about our path, and about our bed, and acquainted with all our ways. He looks into our hearts, and can see each wicked thought and wish. Now, Harry, suppose you begin this year by taking a new shield, to be placed between you and evil thoughts, words, or deeds. The new shield shall be, THOU GOD SEEST ME."

"But will that help me, mother? Oh, it makes me more

afraid, for I am naughty very often. I do want to be a good boy; and I know if I do what is pleasing in God's sight, I cannot displease you and father; but it is very hard, mother."

"Yes, Harry, it is hard, and you need all the more help. Is not God our Father a loving, kind, and merciful Father, who has given his Son to die for us? Should not his service be our pleas‑ure? Does it seem harsh to say, 'A loving Father seeth me?' Children are tempted everyday from the path of duty, at home and at school, at work and at play, and in the house of God. The tempter says, 'Do this thing, though it is forbidden; it won't hurt you. Neglect this duty; no one will find you out. No matter if you do not pray tonight or this morning; nobody will know it.' Then is the time for the new shield to be raised right between yourself and the temptation, whatever it may be—'THOU GOD SEEST ME'—and the wicked thought is not listened to, the wicked word is not spoken, the wicked deed is not committed, for God in love is watching me; he would not that any should perish. Now, Harry, will you take this new shield about with you this New-year? You do not know how it will aid you in your earnest wish to begin right. 'THOU GOD SEEST ME.' Use the shield aright, not as if God were a cruel master whose anger you dreaded, but a loving friend, a watchful parent."

"Oh, mother, this is something to think about. When tempted to do wrong, I can say, Where is my new shield, 'Thou God seest me?' Knowing that he is near, how can I dare to disobey?"

Children, will you not add this new shield to your Christian armor this year? Use it skillfully, that the enemy may not harm you. It will prove an ever-present help. God, who neither slum‑bers nor sleeps, is caring for you by night and by day. Do not offend or disobey him. The Savior calls you, Come to me; and the Spirit will aid all your humble endeavors.

VINEYARD WORK.

DID you ever see a vineyard? Perhaps not; but you have read about vineyards in the Bible and in books of travel. We have orchards and cornfields, not vineyards. There are, however, a few in this country. Mr. Longworth of Cincinnati has vineyards by the acre; and if you should visit him at harvest-time, you would see clusters of grapes that would make your mouth water. Vineyards are very valuable. There is first the fresh ripe grapes. Then raisins, which are grapes pressed. Then grape juice, which is wine; and honey of raisins, to spread on bread, instead of butter.

Judea, where the Bible-men lived, was famous for its vineyards. They were generally planted on the side of a hill. A vineyard needs a great deal of work, and a great variety of work, to keep it in order: digging the stones out and loosening the soil, setting out and tending the young plants, pruning the old vines, and watching against enemies: little foxes, rabbits, and squirrels lie in wait to steal in and destroy the tender vines. As early as June the first ripe grapes are to be gathered, and so on till September, when the general vintage takes place. It is such a happy time then: men, women, and children work together, lightening their labors with songs and merry-making.

Now the Lord Jesus says, "Go work today in my vineyard." Does he say it to us; you and me? Yes, to every one, old and young. Has the Lord Jesus a vineyard? Where is it? It is his church. That is the Lord Jesus' vineyard. There are his choice vines, and the dear little tender plants he cares so much for. He loves it dearly. His church is like a vineyard in many ways, but I speak now of only *one* way: the *great variety and plenty of work* to be done in it. Enough for everybody.

What is vineyard work? Angels are doing it when they fly off on errands of love. Ministers are doing it when they preach the blessed gospel. Missionaries are doing it when they go and tell the poor heathen the way of salvation. What a vineyard worker Dr. Judson was! Sabbath-school teachers are doing it in their endeavors to bring little children into the fold of the Good Shepherd. Tract distributers are doing it when they point poor sinners to the blood of Christ. That was Harlan Page's vineyard work.

You know there are many kinds of work necessary to be done, and they do not interfere with each other. Our hearts should be vines in this vineyard, which we should try to cultivate for God; rooting up bad habits, setting out good ones, nursing virtues, watering feeble graces, watching against sly little sins which creep in like foxes unawares to nibble and destroy much good, sorrow for every cross word, striving to correct a bad disposi‐ tion, speaking gentle and forgiving words: all these, and much more which I could tell you of, are vineyard work. Some little girls were once playing together. Mary flew into a sudden passion, and bit Jenny's arm. Jenny's arm smarted with pain, and she quickly left the room. Nurse presently followed her, and where do you think nurse found the little girl? On her knees before a chair, praying God to forgive Mary for biting her, and to make her good. That little girl, I am sure, was doing *her* bit of vineyard work.

Visiting the poor, kind attentions to the sick, befriending the widow and fatherless, are parts of this good work. Tom, a little boy, had five cents given him to buy some marbles with. Going down street, he saw a poor child stopping before a shop window crying. Tom stopped before the shop window too, and looked in; for he thought maybe she saw something that made her cry, and he wanted to know what it was. But he saw nothing except a sheet of buns, some little cakes, and a few loaves of bread. It could not be those. So he asked her in a kind tone what the matter was. "I'm very hungry," said the poor child; "father is sick, and can't buy enough to eat, and mother won't let us beg." "Oh," thought Tom as he went along, "it was those buns." As he went on, something seemed to whisper, "Feed the hungry;" and as if it was Jesus, instantly it came into his mind how Jesus wrought two big miracles on purpose to do that same thing. His hand went into his pocket; that five cent piece was to buy marbles, "my marbles," he said. "No; let the marbles go. I'll do like Jesus;" and back he ran to the shop, went in, and bought two buns for four cents, which he gave to the child. Oh, how glad she looked! Tommy kept that look in his mind a great while. It did him more good than twice five cents' worth of marbles. That was his vineyard work.

Oh, what good work it is. What pleasant work it is. I hope many dear children are doing it. Are not you?

THE INFANT JESUS.

HOW did anybody know that Jesus, who was born in a stable, was the Son of God? That night, while shepherds were tending their flocks in the fields, a bright angel came to them. They were much afraid at first. "Fear not," said the angel; "I have good news for you. God has sent his Son from heaven to save you from your sins. He is a babe now in a manger at Bethlehem." Then a great many angels in the sky began to sing songs of praise to God for his great goodness to man. The shep-herds left their sheep, and ran to Bethlehem to find the child; and when they saw him, they told everybody that it was the Son of God. How did they know? people asked. The angels told them, they said. How surprised people were.

Not long after, some wise men from a great distance came to Jerusalem. They asked, "Where is the Son of God? We have brought him rich presents, for he is a king." How did they know he was born? God hung a new star in the sky, and bade them follow it. When King Herod heard what they came for, he was much troubled. He called the learned men together, and asked if God had told where his Son was to be born. They said, "Yes; in the town of Bethlehem," for it was so written in the Scrip-tures. Then the king secretly sent for the wise men and told them, and he said, "When you have found him, bring me word, that I may go and worship him also."

The wise men left, and followed the star until it stopped over a house in Bethlehem; and they went in, and found the young child and Mary his mother. Very, very glad were they. And they gave him their presents, and fell down before him, and praised and worshipped him. God told them in a dream not to go back and tell Herod, but to go home some other way.

God knew that Herod did not love his Son, or mean to worship

him. Herod was a very wicked man, and did not want anybody
to be king but himself, not even the Son of God. He wanted to
kill this babe. He was angry when he found the wise men did
not come back to tell him. And what did he do? He ordered his

soldiers to kill all the little children in Bethlehem, sure that Jesus must be one of them. What a bloody day must that have been. Poor little babes! poor mothers and fathers, to have so cruel a king to reign over them. Was Jesus killed? Oh, no; God took care of his Son. He sent word in the night, by an angel, to Joseph and Mary, to arise and leave the town, and take their child to a safe place. They did; they left the country, and did not come back until Herod was dead.

THE CHILD COLPORTEUR.

"MOTHER, will you promise me something?" asked a little boy, laying his hand on his mother's shoulder as she sat busily sewing. "Promise you what?" asked she. "Will you *only* say Yes, mother?" "That would be very rash; you do not want me to say Yes in the dark, do you, Eben?" "Oh but you had just as lief* say so, I know," persisted the child.

"Then I am sure you had just as lief tell me what you want me to say Yes to," said the mother. "Well, then, may I be a *real* colporteur? may I, mother, please?" asked the boy, looking earnestly into her face.

"A real colporteur, Eben?"

"Why, the other day when I stayed at home sick, I played colporteur; shall I show you how? You make believe be a poor woman in a log cabin, mother, and I will come in."

Eben went out; his mother sewed on, when, by and by, a knock was heard at the door. "Come in," said she. The door opened, and in walked the make-believe colporteur, with his old great-coat on, his cap over his ears, and a bag of books slung over his shoulders. "Would you not please to like a good Christian book, ma'am?" said the make-believe colporteur; "one that would do your heart good?"

"I do not know as I should," the old woman in the log cabin seemed to answer.

"Oh, I'll tell you about them, then you'll be very thankful I've come." He took down his bag and opened it. "Here is Little Henry and his Bearer†, there is hardly anything to equal it;" turning over the leaves of the little book, and thrusting them up in her face. "Little Henry was a white heathen; he did not know

*Lief—gladly or willingly.
†Bearer—a house servant.

about God; he was fretful and very naughty. Neither his mother nor father, nobody told him about Jesus. He was left to his poor heathen bearer, who taught him to worship idols. By and by a young lady from England told little Henry of Jesus, and then Henry told his bearer. As his bearer carried him all around, Henry talked beautifully to him. He told him how Jesus loved the poor heathen, and died to save them. Then his bearer too became a Christian. Then he was happy; he was not happy before. Is it not pretty? Oh it is good; I think you had better take it."

"But suppose I am too poor to buy?"

"Then you shall have it for nothing, if you will read it, and mind all the bearer says. It is as good as preaching: please take it;" and the make-believe colporteur put the book into the hands of the make-believe woman of the log cabin.

"There, mother," Eben then exclaimed, shoving back his cap, "cannot I be a *real* colporteur? Why, mother," he went on to say, while a deep seriousness overspread his face, "did you know there are a great many very wicked folks down behind this street? The little children swear awfully. I asked them if they had any good books, and they said No. Is not this a good place for a colporteur, mother; and ought we not to do something for them? Could not *I* be a colporteur, mother? I am not too little, am I?"

"Where can you get books, Eben?" asked she.

"Why, have not I got some? Jane can give me a few, and Susan— perhaps you and father will be glad to help. Don't you think, mother, we can spare our books? we have read them through and through: why, you know we *ought* to try to do good with them."

The mother was very much pleased with the plan, and when he begged to begin next Saturday afternoon, she gave her consent. How interested was Eben collecting and assorting his little books; this would do best, and that had the ten commandments in it, and another was about lying: he looked them all over, and could tell what each was about. When Saturday afternoon came, his mother thought he might forget it, for his brothers loved play, and always wanted Eben to go with them; but no, Eben took no interest in bat and ball upon the common;

he had another plan which he liked better; so he packed his little books into a basket and set forth.

"Goodbye, Mr. Colporteur," exclaimed Jane. His mother took a tender interest in all his proceedings; she did not hinder him, for she thought haply the Lord has sent him; and when she watched him go forth so serious and so earnest, she bade him God-speed in her heart, and prayed that the gracious Savior might please to bless these humble doings.

Eben was gone a long while; and when at last he came back, he had many things to tell his mother. "Why, mother," said he, "all the mothers were as glad as could be; and some of the little children that could not read, I read to them. There was one big boy who swore, mother," said the child, fixing his large eyes upon her: "I told him about the third commandment. I told him God would punish swearers; I told him I would bring him a book about it."

Was not the mission of this child-colporteur a beautiful one? I have thought how many nurseries and book-cases there are in Christian homes piled up with books, read and reread for the last time, laid away and cast aside, which are not yet too old to be useful, and which might be threading their way to the alleys of ignorance and sin; and I have wondered if children, dear Christian children, in their simplicity and earnestness, might not go forth to the poor, ragged, vicious children of their neighborhoods, and carry to them the bread and water of life.

Ah, children, do you not often abuse books? Is not a cover gone from one, and have you not torn up the stray leaf of another, without thinking, minding or caring about it? Stop a moment, and think if these good little books may not be of use still: you have read and loved them: are there not many, many others who would love to read them too? On some bright Wednesday after-noon can you not forsake your play, your dolls, or your skates, and gather up a little store of neglected books for the destitute corners and alleys of your neighborhood—as destitute as the log-cabin on the distant prairie? Can you not become a child-colporteur? Oh, it would be a delightful and blessed service, thus to follow Him who "went about doing good."

MISS GREY AND THE RUDE BOY.

MISS Grey's school was in the outskirts of a village, in a lonely by-place, where the children were rude and ignorant. The school was called a hard school, because the scholars, not being properly governed at home, hated to mind their teachers. Miss Grey was warned not to go. "They'll turn you out the first week," her friends said. But Miss Grey said she would try; she was indeed not easily frightened or discouraged. The scholars did not turn her out the first week; but she learned a good deal about the scholars, and they learned a good deal about her; and she found it was not so very hard a school, after all. In truth, she did not take it to have an easy time, or merely to get her wages; she went to do the children good. She loved the Lord Jesus, and she remembered how he said, "Feed my lambs;" and she knew these children were *his* lambs, only they had always been *stray* lambs; and she thought how happy she should be to lead these little stray lambs back to Jesus' good fold. Was she not a kind schoolmistress? The children began to love her dearly.

Now there was one boy worse than the rest. He would not mind; he would not study; he seemed to take pleasure in giving trouble to others; he did not care for anybody. He often boasted "*he* did not care for mistress." And for a long time the mistress could not find any little soft place in his heart to touch him; she thought for a long time there must be such a place, for she could not believe the boy's heart could be all hard, and yet she could not find it.

Then she thought she would go over to the boy's home, and see his home and his father and mother. It was a long walk through the woods, and not a very nice looking hut when she found it. His mother was at home, and some of the neighbors were in. "Well,

mistress, what do you make of our jackanapes?* He is a mis-
chievous little cur as ever was," said the mother in a rough
tone. "I tell him he'll come to the gallows some time." The

---

*Jackanapes—a rude person.

mistress did not tell all she thought; she only spoke as kindly as she could; and after staying a little while, she set out for home.

"Dick, you cur, go and show the mistress the shortest way." Dick, who was perched on the wood-pile, jumped down. He whistled, and then walked on. He whistled again. "Who are you whistling for?" asked the mistress. "For my dog," answered Dick. "Ah, you never told me you had a dog. I like dogs. I should like to see your dog;" and Miss Grey told about her dog at home. Soon they came to a fork in the road. "There," said Dick, "you take the right road, and you'll get home. A'n't 'fraid, are you?" Miss Grey said she was not, and Dick took to his heels home.

Miss Grey thought he left quite on a sudden; but it was only Dick after all, and she walked on alone and thinking. It was not long, however, before she heard a running behind her. She looked around, and lo, there was Dick and his dog in hot haste after her. "I brought my dog to show you," he said. "Mother hates dogs, and father hates *mine*; but he and I like each other the best of any. Here, Watch; here, sir, speak to the mistress. A'n't he a beauty, mistress?" Mistress had certainly seen handsomer dogs; but she spoke kindly to Watch, and Watch wagged his tail, very much pleased. Dick and Watch trudged quite home with her. It was a very sociable walk.

The next morning Dick came to school in season, and he took his slate and tried to cipher his lesson. "I like mistress first-rate," he told the boys; and from that time Miss Grey had no trouble with Dick. In fact, she found the soft place in his heart; she *sympathized* with him about his dog. Poor Dick's parents forgot they had ever been children. They had been hard with the boy; they had never sympathized with him in his child interests and trials and pleasures. Miss Grey felt for children. She remembered when she was a child, and poor Dick thought he never had found before such a friend in his life. How he now began to improve.

It is this power of sympathy with us that makes the Lord Jesus such a precious friend. He "became flesh," that is, became a child and a man, not only that he might die for sinners, but that he might *feel* for us. We are so apt to forget this. If we thought of it oftener, we should often fly to him for comfort and help. In one thing he is different from every other friend. He does not judge by the greatness of the trial or sorrow which disturbs us, but by its effect upon us. To him, nothing is insignificant which affects us. He can sympathize just as much with the tears of a little child at an unkind word, as with a poor man for the loss of his house. "For we have not a High-priest who cannot be touched with the feeling of our infirmities; but was in all points tempted like as we are, yet without sin." Heb. 4:15.

GOLD-APPLE WORDS.

THERE are some words, the Bible says, which are "like apples of gold in pictures of silver." Many suppose this phrase would be better translated *baskets* of silver; but it does not matter much. The point is, that there are some words as precious and beautiful as gold apples in silver baskets. What words can they be? for there are many kinds—idle words, careless words, cross words, wicked words, words of counsel and of caution, parting words, flattering words. Ah, none of these; but a *"word fitly spoken."*

The gold-apple word then is a fit word. It fits the occasion. It fits the truth. Love and kindness fit it. What a precious word it must be. So it is.

A man in prison once fell sick. He was a very wicked man, a murderer, and the kind doctor who visited him tried to do something for his poor soul as well as his body. He asked pious friends also to call on the prisoner and talk with him. They tried to make him see his guilt in the sight of God, and the willingness of Christ to receive even the worst who come to him. Nothing, however, made any impression. He seemed completely hardened. By and by a good old man visited the cell; and this is the account the prisoner gave of it.

"Doctor," he said, when the doctor came in, "you don't understand how. You want to do good to our souls, but you don't go about it right. You keep saying, Repent, repent! just as if we didn't know that before. But that dear old man knew how. He came in and sat down right beside me. He looked good, and with an eye full of tenderness, he said to me, 'John, wasn't it gracious goodness on the part of the Almighty that he should have loved *us* so much as to send his only begotten and well-beloved Son into the world to save such sinners as you and *I?*'

Why, doctor, that word *I* killed me; it killed me dead. I couldn't get over it, that that good man should put himself on the *same level with me*, a wicked murderer, neither fit to live nor fit to die. I cannot keep it out of my mind."

He never could. It sunk deep. His heart was touched, and it ended in the poor man's fleeing to Christ for pardon. "Never," said the doctor, "did I witness a greater change that when poor John ——, the murderer, turned Christian and died so peace·ably." Those were indeed "*fitly chosen*," gold-apple words.

You remember Naaman the great Syrian general took cap·tive a little Jewish maid, and he carried her home and gave her to his wife. The child did not forget her pious education, but she loved and feared God. Naaman was sick of a dreadful and dangerous disease. Nobody could help him. "Would God my lord was with the prophet that is in Samaria, for he would cure him," said the little maid to her mistress. Her mistress told it to her husband, and Naaman took a journey to Samaria, and he saw the prophet of God, and he believed in his word and was healed. Those were gold-apple words of the little maid.

A poor woman lost her husband, and she took on piteously, afraid lest her little family might be pinched with want. "Isn't our heavenly Father living, mother?" asked her little son. Indeed he is. She forgot, but he remembered; and her little boy's gold-apple words comforted her.

Ah, they drop not from the wise and grown up only; small lips speak them, and they then seem sweeter than ever. We should try to have none others in our families. Home should be full of them. There is no other spot so full of opportunities for words of truth, of love, and of kindness. They fit everywhere, upstairs and down, in the kitchen and the parlor.

Scarce as gold is, and fruit also, we may each of us have our "apples of gold in silver baskets." They are beautiful and pre·cious, "sweeter than honey or the honeycomb." Do not fail of a good supply, and give them to everybody as you have opportu·nity, dear child.

THE GREAT COMMANDER.

BOYS, do you want to enlist? Should you like to be a soldier? But first count the cost. Soldiers, at best, have hard times of it. They leave father and mother, brothers and sisters, wives and children. They are exposed to all sorts of weather, hot or cold, wet or dry. They can't choose their times or seasons. They have hard fare. Often they have short rations, sleep on the damp ground, or have no sleep at all. They are liable to be blown up by bomb-shells, or have their limbs shot off by cannon-balls, or fall by the bayonet. Thirty men once offered their services to a captain. "If you enlist under me, half of you will be dead men before thirty days," said he. "Aye, aye, sir," answered the men; for brave men never flinch at danger. War, with all its great evils, has called out shining virtues. Nothing demands greater sacrifice. The mother gives her boy, rich men part with their money, and thousands give themselves. Nor is it done for "the pay." A soldier's pay is poor pay, only a few dollars a month, not half the wages of a farm-hand; but it is willingly, cheerfully met and undergone at the call of duty.

The *children* are called for. Will you not enlist? "Are we called to fight?" Yes. There is a Commander who invites, nay, who is urgent for the children to join him in his march. He has a soldier's suit for you. It is not red and gold, like our uniform, or brass and iron, like the old Romans'; but it is a glorious fit. And a sword too. You shall be fully armed and equipped, depend upon that. Come, come; duty calls you. You will have to fight; there is no dodging it; but it will be a "good fight." And perhaps I ought to say, to comfort you, that the Captain *never lost a man who obeyed orders*. Washington could not say that. Much as he felt for his poor soldiers, he could not save them from a soldier's fate. Napoleon left his thousands on every battle-field. But the Captain who would recruit his ranks from the children, can with strict truth say, "Of them which thou gavest me *I have lost none*." Think of that. What other commander could ever say it? Yet mind this, *you must obey orders*. But can he make his *words good*? Yes. "All his commandments are sure; *they stand fast for ever and ever*; they are done in truth."

Who is this great Captain? What is his name? Jesus Christ. Satan is your bitter enemy, determined to seize you. He goes about like a "roaring lion." "The fiery darts of the wicked" are pointed at you, while the traitor Sin is at the very door of your heart. God pitied you. He sent his Son, his well-beloved Son to save you. "Behold," says God, "I have given him for a leader and commander to the people." "Seek ye him while he may be found; call upon him while he is near."

Jesus Christ came. He suffered for us; he died for us on the cross; but he now lives and reigns, and has set up his standard, which is called the "Standard of the Cross." Have you seen his proclamation? This is a part of it: "Ho, every one; incline your ear, and come unto me; hear, and your soul shall live." "No weapon that is formed against thee shall prosper; ye shall go out with joy, and be led forth with peace." Will you not serve? Here is your soldier's suit: the "breastplate of righteousness and the shield of faith and the helmet of salvation and the sword of the Spirit, which is the word of God." Put this on, and you are armed for the fight—a fight not with "flesh and blood," but against sin and Satan—a fight for Christ's glorious kingdom within and without you, worth braving and daring everything for. It is well called "the good fight."

Sometimes you find the soldiers of Christ looking quite poor, and proud people say they have poor pay. Ah, they don't know. Besides his daily rations from a treasury always full—for the silver and the gold and the cattle on a thousand hills belong to Christ—every faithful soldier has a final reward. What? "Be thou faithful unto death, and I will give thee a crown of life," says the Commander to every one who enlists. Every little child even shall *wear a crown*. Nobody but kings and queens wear crowns upon earth. They are very costly, and very splendid. Millions of dollars and millions of lives have been spent to win and wear a crown. Yet Christ promises one to every faithful soldier—a "crown of life"—something very, very precious laid up in heaven. Come, dear child, come to Christ; come and enlist a soldier of the cross. The martial music of this host runs thus:

> Am I a soldier of the cross,
>   A follower of the Lamb?
> And shall I fear to own his cause,
>   Or blush to speak his name?
>
> Sure I must fight if I would reign:
>   Increase my courage, Lord;
> I'll bear the toil, endure the pain,
>   Supported by thy word.

A STRAYING TESTAMENT.

I WANT to show you how the Bible is making its way into the heart of the Turkish Empire. Let us visit Sivas, a city perched among the mountains of Asia Minor. There are no railroads, or steamboats, or coaches, or trains of any description in that country. You must clamber over their rough roads on horse or mule-back, carrying your goods and luggage in saddle-bags.

Very odd-looking villages you will come to. The houses are built of earth, with only two rooms and one outside door. One room is for the donkies, cows, and dogs, while the family live in the other on very sociable terms with these animals. Almost every village has a "guest-house," built by some pious Turk for the accommodation of travelers. Here you will find fire to warm you, and food to eat.

Sivas is a large inland city about eighteen hours from Tocat. And how far is eighteen hours? you will ask. Eighteen hours is about fifty miles, which makes comfortable travelling about three miles an hour; rather slow going for a Yankee. It has fifty thousand inhabitants, Turks, Greeks, and Armenians. Within two or three years Bible Christianity has taken root there; and the Scriptures are kept publicly for sale in four different parts of the city. These are in the Turkish and Greek languages. Mr. Righter, an agent of the American Bible Society, paid a visit to this city a few months ago, and held a Bible meeting in the little mission chapel. In the afternoon, two of the Koozelbesh Koords from a village twelve hours distant called upon him. The Koords, you know, are mountain men, and one of the fiercest tribes in Asia. One of them was the son of a sheik, or chief man of the village. They said they wanted to become gospel Christians. "Why do you want to change your religion?" asked Mr. Righter. "We once worshipped a cane or staff," they said, "with which the sheik beat us, to drive away our sins. We used to meet once a week to receive this beating. Then we confessed our sins, and yearly offered a sacrifice of sheep to the cane. We no longer believe this will save us. A kitab," good book, "taught us better."

"Where did you get the book?" asked the missionary. "We don't know where it came from," they answered; "but it teaches us that Christ is alive, and the other prophets are dead. It teaches us to love our enemies, and to pray for them. It is ten years since we began to learn these truths." "What is the name of the book?" "We call it Boyusook," book of command, they said. "A khojah, or teacher, reads to us from this book, the sheik explains it, and then we pray to God through Christ, as the book teaches."

Then the missionary told them he called it "Ingil," the gospel of salvation, and how many copies of this book there were in America. They wished very much to have a missionary come and comfort and teach them, for the savage Koords were very angry with them for loving the book; and they often beat and robbed them of their flocks, because they would not worship idols as they used to. They also said there were hundreds more ready to receive the gospel, but for fear of their enemies.

The missionaries bade them keep up a good heart, for God would stand by those who put their trust in him. "Go back," said the missionary, "to your native village, and boldly preach this gospel of love and salvation, even to your cruelest persecutors." "Inshallah!" God be praised, they both exclaimed.

Such is the influence of a stray copy of the Testament, which found its solitary way through the rocky passes of Asia Minor, teaching these Koords the folly of idol-worship, and leading them to "the Lamb of God, who taketh away the sin of the world." Who will not give, if he can give no more, one Testament to the poor heathen?

THE DROWNED GOD.

IN the valley of Godovey, in India, there lived a little heathen boy called Tookaram. Tookaram was quite religious in his way. His father and mother were dead, and they left him to a poor widow, who took pity on him, and called him her son. This woman was a devotee. A devotee is one who thinks the performance of rites and ceremonies will save the soul. She spent her time in visiting holy places, praying to a great many idols, and lived by begging. The Hindoos are fond of giving to such beggars, because they expect to be paid in prayers. Little Tookaram went with his new mother, and, as I said, was quite a religious little boy in his way.

A missionary one day met Tookaram, and asked him to come to his school and learn to read. That pleased the little fellow very much; for he wanted to learn to read. So early the next day, with a loaf of bread on his head, for it was some distance, he started off for the missionary's school. On his way, he came to the bank of a river, where many people were collected, and they seemed to be in great trouble. What was the matter? Had somebody that could not swim fallen in? Was anybody drowned? The river was swollen by a night rain, and was very high and angry. Yes, somebody had. Oh, poor fellow; who? Why, it was a god that had tumbled in, and he could not swim any better than a stone; so half the village had turned out to fish him up. They had got a rope round his neck, and were pulling and shouting with all their might; but to no purpose. They could not save him, any more than he could save them. They must leave him to his fate, or wait till the river went down and then drag him out with oxen.

Little Tookaram stopped and looked at this strange sight with wonder. He then stripped off his clothes, piled them on his head, plunged boldly into the stream, and swam to the other side, where the missionary's school was. How much more power he had in the water than the god! The little stranger was kindly welcomed at the school. After his bashfulness wore off, and he became acquainted with the scholars, he told them about the drowned god.

"Oh," said the little boys at school, "he is not a God; he is an idol. He is a made god: he has eyes, but he sees not; he has ears, but he hears not; he has a mouth, but he speaks not; he knows nothing, and he can't help those who pray to him any better than he can help himself: he is it *dead* god. He is not *our* God; our God is the *living* God;" for the Hindoo children of the missionary school had learned to worship the Christian's God, the Lord of heaven and earth.

"Who is your God?" asked little Tookaram. "Jehovah," answered the children, "the Maker and Father of everything." "Where does he live?" asked Tookaram. "He is a Spirit," answered the children; "he lives everywhere, he sees everybody, he knows everything." Little Tookaram was filled with amazement. A drowned god did not indeed seem like a God to worship and pray to. His poor little brain was full of painful and puzzling ideas; but a great, new thought had got lodged there: a *living* God, instead of the dead gods, idols of wood and stone, which he had before worshipped. Then he learned that God so loved this world, that he sent his dear Son to save us from our sins, and that he died on the cruel cross to do it. Tookaram tore the beads from his neck and declared himself a Christian. He began to pray to God, and the Holy Spirit enlightened his mind and melted his heart, and he became a heartfelt believer in Bible truth.

By and by his adopted mother hears of it, and comes to the school very angry. She is determined to take Tookaram away. But the lovely Christian spirit of the missionary and his household quiets her. The tale of her little son too has a strange pleasantness in it. It is Tookaram, and it is not Tookaram. Christian Tookaram is not the heathen Tookaram. She stays and stays to hear more, and the Holy Spirit, little by little, opens her blinded eyes to see the blessed truth, and at last she finds in Jesus Christ all she has been ever seeking for among the idols of her own land: the burden of her sins rolled away; pardon and peace to her poor soul.

Some months after this, Tookaram and his mother stood up, with five others, in a small Christian congregation in India, and publicly professed their faith in Jesus Christ.

JOPPA.

THERE is a place in the land of Palestine, on the seacoast, about forty miles north-west of Jerusalem, which the people now living in that country call *Yaffa*. It is the same place that is called Joppa in the Bible, and is a very old town.

I woke up one morning very early, when I was travelling in a steamer on the Mediterranean Sea, and found myself in front of this old city. It was the first time that I had looked upon the Holy Land. The steamer was lying at anchor some distance from the shore, and I observed four or five sharp jagged rocks near by, which rose above the water, and which seemed to me to make the place rather dangerous for vessels in a storm. There is no harbor here, and when the wind blows briskly from the west, the waves dash over these rocks and against the shore with great violence. Close to the water's edge stands the city. It is not on level ground, but occupies a high and abrupt hill, which rises directly from the shore, about one hundred and fifty feet high. This hill, shaped somewhat like a flat sugar-loaf, is completely covered on the top and on the steep sides by the irregular white stone houses of the city. It is true this is a queer place for a city containing five thousand inhabitants, but I suppose they built this city on a hill because they found it necessary sometimes to defend themselves against the attacks of robbers and enemies; for people on a high place can fight in their own defense to better advantage than on a plain.

When I landed from the steamer, in a little boat, the wind was not blowing very strong, but the waves clashed over the rocks along the shore, and high up against the houses at the water's edge. I found the streets very crooked, and some of them so narrow that two children, joining hands in the middle of the street, might touch with their other hands the houses on

both sides. Some of the streets too are very steep, often requir·
ing stone stairs for people to walk up and down. I saw a little
donkey with a very large sack of barley on his back, walking
carefully down one of these long stairways. A little further on, I
saw a great ugly-looking grey animal, very tall and long-legged,
with a long crooked neck, and small flat head, and short ears.
What animal do you suppose this was? It was a camel, and his
master had just put upon his back two enormous boxes, one on
each side, to carry to Jerusalem.

In the north-west part of the city, on the level ground, I saw
the *Bazaar*. Do you ask what this is? It is the name which is
given to that street where all the stores and shops of the city
are collected together, and where are to be seen at all hours of
the day a great many people. The stores are little square places
or rooms on each side of the narrow street, open on the front
side, and filled with all kinds of goods. In these places, and
along the street, was a crowd of people, who were lounging
about and appeared to have nothing to do. Some were standing,
but most were sitting on the ground and on benches, cross-
legged, and nearly all were smoking long pipes. They did not
wear coats and pantaloons,* like people in this country, but had
on long robes or frocks, which came down almost to their feet,
and were kept in place by girdles around the body. Instead of
hats, they wore long strips of white cloth wrapped around the
head many times, which they call *turbans*. There were also, here
and there, a few women; but their faces were closely covered by
long narrow veils, which concealed all the face except the eyes.

I went out into the open space outside the city, and here I
saw a great many camels lying resting on the ground, some
with only their clumsy saddles on their backs, others all loaded
ready for a journey. On both sides of the roads outside the city
are fences composed of cactus, or prickly pear, which grows so
high that a man riding on horseback could not look over the top.
But I could look through the spaces between the thick branches
and leaves, and see the beautiful gardens filled with orange-
trees, which were hanging with ripe yellow fruit. There were

---

*Pantaloon—trousers.

also almond and pomegranate trees, and many other trees the names of which sounded very strange. These spacious gardens extend all around the north-eastern and eastern parts of the city, but on the southern side are heaps of barren sand, and no cultivation.

Do you ask what there was about this queer old city that interested me so much? It was the fact that Joppa is mentioned so many times in the Bible. It existed in the days of Joshua, more than three thousand years ago, and fell by lot to the tribe of Dan. It is the place where King Solomon landed the timber from the sea, which he brought from Mount Lebanon, when he was building the temple in Jerusalem. From Joppa, Jonah set sail when he fled from the face of the Lord. It is the place where Dorcas lived, who made so many garments for the poor, and whom Peter raised to life after she had died. And it was the place where the apostle Peter was lodging, at the time he saw the remarkable vision which you may read about in the tenth chapter of Acts.

When I was returning into the city from my long walk, my guide took me to an old ruin by the sea-side, in the southern part of the city, which an uncertain tradition points out as the site of the house of Simon the tanner, where Peter lodged. Many people, especially pilgrims to the Holy Land, visit this spot, and believe that it is the very place where the apostle saw the vision. Whether this is the place or not, I cannot tell. But it seemed very strange to me that so many poor people should leave their homes, and travel thousands of miles, exposing themselves to great privations and dangers, in the belief that by suffering so much in order to look upon the so-called Holy Places, they would be sure of the favor of God. I am sure the road to heaven does not lie through such pilgrimages and sufferings as these. Christ has suffered once for all, and has borne our sins on the cross. He accepts only the humble and contrite heart. He will hear sincere prayer, even from a little child, when it is offered up to him in simple faith. He listens with a ready ear to all your cries. It makes no difference where you are. He catches the accents of humble faith just as readily in your quiet chamber when you kneel by your bedside at night, as though you knelt down upon the stones where the blessed apostles walked, or the Savior suffered and died.

A LITTLE TALK.

THREE little girls were telling each other one evening what they wanted to be. One wanted to be a queen; another to write books. The third said she should be contented to be a lamb in Christ's fold. Ah, that was the *greatest* as well as the *best* wish of all. The *greatest*, and yet the *easiest* to be had; for Christ says, "Come;" and what have we to do but to *go*?

"Suppose you stray away and get lost," said one of the others.

"The Son of man is come to seek and to save that which was lost," replied she.

Oh yes, we should never find Christ if he did not find us. We should never seek him if he did not seek us first. Sometimes sheep and lambs get lost in the snow-storms, and the shepherd sets out and seeks them, and finds them in the deep ravines, huddled together under the snow. He digs the snow away, but they are afraid to stir. They won't take a single step to save their lives; so the good shepherd *carries* them out. Thus Jesus saves his lost sheep. He finds them in the deep pit of sin. They can't help themselves; so he reaches out his strong arm, and takes them out.

Jesus *provides* for his sheep and lambs. "They go in and out, and find pasture." You may be sure of being fed if you are Christ's lamb. You shall have bread to eat and clothes to wear. "I have been young, and now am old," says King David, "yet have I never seen the righteous forsaken, nor his seed begging bread." Christ is always able to pasture his flock. His pastures never dry up, or are burnt over. He also feeds their souls. Did you ever see the little flower fed by the morning dew? Just so will Christ feed you with the dews of his grace and love. The *Bible* is a table-full—a rich feast to the hungry soul. You can feed on its leaves everyday, three times a day, all through the year, and all through the years of the longest life that ever was, and yet they never fail. There is enough and to spare; and what is better, you *never* get tired of it. It tastes better and better everyday.

I know of nobody that would die for me. Do you? But "the good Shepherd giveth his life for his sheep." All that are in Christ's flock were once condemned to die. Jesus pitied them. He left his Father's house, and came into this wicked world to die for them. "While we were yet sinners, Christ died for us." Therefore every sheep and every little lamb can say, "He loved me, and gave himself for me."

Oh, how precious to be a lamb in Christ's fold! The greatest, the best, the easiest reached of all wishes is—to be there.

THE DYING SOLDIER.

A YOUNG soldier was shot on the battle-field, and dragged by a comrade aside to die. He shut his eyes, and all his past life flashed before him. It seemed but an instant of time. He looked forward and saw *eternity*, like a great gulf, ready to swallow him up, with his sins as so many weights sinking him deeper and deeper.

Suddenly a lesson which his pious mother taught him when a little boy at her knee, stood before him in shining letters. It was a lesson he heard repeated again and again and again; she was never tired of imprinting it on his memory before she died; it was her only legacy. In the gayety of life he had forgotten it. He had lost his hold on it, but it had never quite lost its hold on him; and now, in this hour of peril, it threw out to him a rope of mercy. What was it? "God so loved the world, that he gave his only begotten Son, that whosoever believeth in him should not perish, but have eternal life."

He caught the rope; it seemed let down from heaven. "Lord, I believe," he cried; "save me, or I perish!"

Till he died, a few hours after, he said little but this one prayer: "Lord, I believe; save me, or I perish!" a prayer never uttered by the penitent soul in vain.

That was a lesson worth more than all the gold of earth.

www.ingramcontent.com/pod-product-compliance
Lightning Source LLC
Chambersburg PA
CBHW021044130626
46552CB00005B/2008